The Long Road Home

Karen Brooks

Copyright *All rights reserved* ©

Year of publication: 2025

Author's Name: Karen Sharon BROOKS

Edition: 0002025001

ISBN: 9798280142572

Imprint: Independently published

First print: April 2025

Special Thanks

A heartfelt thank you to **Alvin Tang**, who is not only my husband but also my biggest supporter. Your guidance, patience and unwavering encouragement have been invaluable throughout this journey. From helping me refine my words to assisting in the publishing process, your belief in this book has made it possible.

Dedication

"This book is dedicated to my beloved mother, Sylvia whose remarkable life journey inspired this story. Your resilience, strength and love have shaped the person I am today. This is a tribute to the struggles you faced, the sacrifices you made, and the unwavering spirit you carried through it all. May your story continue to inspire others, just as it has inspired me.

This book is also dedicated to my friends, whose positive words and steadfast belief in my writing have kept me going. Your encouragement has been a constant source of light and support throughout this journey."

Quote

"In the face of adversity, it's the love we give and the faith others have in us that helps us find the courage to keep going."

Karen Brooks

Table of Contents

Preface

Every story begins with a seed, an idea, a memory, or an event that grows into something much larger than we ever imagined. The Long Road Home is one such story, born from the deep well of history, love, loss and the unbreakable strength of the human spirit.

Born in 1942, during the upheaval of World War II, Marica's life was marked by the Japanese invasion of Singapore. The hardships faced by her family during this dark period, including the loss of her father Henry on the battlefield, form the heart of this narrative. Her mother Nancy, a resilient and determined woman, navigates the harsh realities of war, finding a way to survive and protect her daughter. Together, they escape the devastation to find refuge on Pulau Ubin, yet the scars of loss and war remain with them, shaping their futures.

As Marica grows up in 1960s Singapore, she embarks on a journey of love and self-discovery, ultimately falling for Edward, a British Air Force officer. Their romance introduces the complexities of two cultures colliding, East meets West, as Marica's Singaporean heritage and Edward's British upbringing create both tension and beauty within their relationship. The blending of these worlds becomes a key theme, highlighting the challenges of identity, family expectations, and love when two cultures, so different yet so alike, intertwine.

In writing this book, I aimed to capture the unsaid emotions: the silent sacrifices, the strength found in adversity, and the deep love that can flourish even in the darkest times. Marica's journey, shaped by the loss of her father and the strength of her mother, reflects the complexities of relationships, the weight of secrets, and the power of forgiveness. This story is not just about the past. It is about the choices we make, the love we hold onto and the courage it takes to face the unknown.

Thank you for joining me on this emotional journey. As you walk beside Marica, experiencing her pain, triumphs and discoveries, I hope you will find a part of yourself in her story. *The Long Road Home* is a testament to the resilience within us all, the strength to love in the face of loss and the hope that pushes us forward, even in the most challenging times.

Through Marica's journey, you will witness both the weight of war and tragedy, and the incredible power of the human spirit to heal, rebuild, and find light in the darkest of moments. It is a story of discovering strength when all seems broken, of holding onto love despite its challenges, and of confronting the past to create a better future.

This book celebrates the enduring power of hope. Even after unimaginable loss, we can rise, stand strong, and continue forward. It is about embracing the pieces of ourselves that remain after everything changes, and discovering that, in our darkest moments, there is always room for growth, healing, and love.

As you accompany Marica, you will be reminded that life though filled with struggles, is also abundant with second chances, resilience and the capacity to move forward, no matter the scars we carry. May her story inspire you to embrace your own resilience, cherish the love in your life and never lose sight of hope, even when the road ahead seems uncertain.

Karen Brooks

Chapter 1: A Child of War (1942)

Nancy - A Woman of Two Worlds

Nancy Pereira was born in 1917 into a life that seemed like something out of a storybook. The daughter of a well-to-do businessman and his elegant wife, she had grown up in a large white colonial house near Little India. Her family's home was an imposing, stately structure, surrounded by lush gardens and tall gates that kept the outside world at bay. Her father, a man of great ambition, had built his fortune through successful trade deals and Nancy was raised in the comfort of privilege.

She was the youngest of twenty siblings, a mix of full and half-brothers and sisters, each one a thread in the intricate tapestry of her family. Despite the size of the household, Nancy's mother, a soft-spoken woman with a quiet strength, managed to care for each of her children with love and attention. Their home was always bustling with activity, young voices chattering, the smell of chicken curry rice, stir-fried vegetables, and fragrant pandan cakes wafting from the kitchen and the ever-present hum of servants moving about. The air was often filled with the savoury aroma of laksa, satay and kaya toast, creating a warm and inviting atmosphere where family and friends gathered to share meals and memories.

Nancy's childhood had been filled with the luxuries of a life many could only dream of fine silks, grand parties, and a sense of safety.

But beneath the surface, there was always a feeling of distance, an unspoken barrier between Nancy and the world beyond the gates of their home. She had been kept sheltered from the struggles of the outside world. That was until the war came.

Her mother had always told her that the world was unpredictable, but Nancy had never believed it until she saw the skies above Singapore darken with the shadow of enemy bombers.

As a young woman, Nancy had married Henry Tan, a man who came from a much humbler background. He had been a local tradesman, a man of simple tastes and honest labour. They had met by chance at a community event, where Nancy, tired of the constraints of her privileged life, found herself drawn to Henry's quiet confidence and genuine nature. While she had grown up surrounded by luxury and expectation, Henry's warmth and steadiness offered a refreshing contrast. He had caught her attention with a kind smile and an easy laugh, and in the simplicity of their first conversation, Nancy felt something she hadn't known she was missing: a connection grounded in sincerity. She had left the grandeur of her family's house to build a new life with him, first in a small apartment and then later in their humble wooden shack on the outskirts of the city.

Though Nancy had once revelled in the comforts of wealth, she now found herself living in a world stripped of everything she had known. The war had stolen it all, her home, her garden, the family legacy she had cherished for so long. And now, as if to rub salt into the wound, it threatened to take away her daughter, the only piece of her heart that remained untouched. In those quiet, restless nights, when the sounds of battle seemed to echo in her mind, Nancy understood something profound.

The luxuries of her past had once seemed so important, but now she realized that true wealth wasn't measured by what you could hold in your hands. It was measured by the love you held in your heart, the love for the people who meant everything to you. And Marica, her daughter, was that love, her heart, her soul, the very reason she fought to survive.

Henry - The Protector

Henry Tan was not a man of many words. A quiet and resolute figure, he had been the backbone of their family for as long as Nancy could remember. He was a sturdy, well-built man in his early thirties, with thick black hair now starting to show streaks of grey from the stress of the war. His hands, once smooth from trade work, were now calloused and rough, bearing the marks of survival.

Henry had grown up in the heart of Singapore, in a cramped alleyway near the river. His family was poor, but they had always made do, scraping together what they could.

As a boy, he had learned to be resourceful, teaching himself to fix broken tools and repair machines. He had a natural skill for mechanics and had worked his way up from a humble apprentice to a skilled craftsman.

When he met Nancy, he had been working as a tradesman, mending shoes and repairing small household goods. She had caught his eye one afternoon when he was fixing a bicycle in the market. She had stood there, watching him work, her face framed by the warm light of the sun. He had admired her beauty, but more than that, it was her strength that had drawn him to her. There was something about the way she carried herself, so graceful, yet so unaware of her own power, which made him want to protect her.

Together, they had created a life. Nancy had brought a sense of order and calm into his life, while he had given her the love and stability she never truly knew.

But now, in the shadow of war, it was Henry's resolve that would be tested more than ever before.

A Life Interrupted

Before the war, Singapore had been a city of contrasts, a thriving, multi-ethnic hub of trade where East met West. Colonial architecture stood side by side with traditional Malay and Chinese shophouses. The streets were always alive with the sounds of bustling vendors, the scent of street food wafting through the air, and the endless tide of people moving through the city's markets.

The Pereira family's home, a grand white house near Little India, had been a peaceful retreat amidst the vibrant and bustling surroundings. In their lush garden, Nancy's mother would host lavish gatherings where guests sipped sweet tea and enjoyed fine pastries, homemade pineapple jam tarts, delicious curry puffs, and their great-grandmother's cherished Devils Curry recipe, all beneath the shade of tall, swaying palm trees.

The house itself was a colonial masterpiece, its gleaming white façade a symbol of their family's wealth and status. But now, it was a distant memory, a place lost to the ravages of war.

The transition to their small shack on the outskirts of the city had been difficult. Gone were the days of silk curtains and grand dinners; now, their life was reduced to the bare essentials.

The house was simple, a small wooden structure with a tin roof and little more than a few pieces of furniture and personal belongings. But it was a place of comfort, and it had been a haven in the midst of chaos.

Now, as the war raged on outside their door, even this small refuge was not safe.

Nancy's memories of that grand house were like faded photographs, beautiful, but increasingly distant. The bustling streets of Little India, where the air had once been thick with the scents of incense and curry, now felt like a lifetime ago. The war had stolen everything from her, leaving her with only the most basic instincts to survive.

The sounds of gunfire and explosions had drowned out the joyful noise of children playing in the streets. The lively markets that once bustled with life now lay in ruins, their charred remnants serving as a testament to the devastation wrought by the Japanese invasion.

Nancy could still vividly recall the last time she had seen their home; the moment they were forced to flee as Japanese soldiers marched through the city. She remembered the white walls, the lush gardens, the warmth of the life they had once known. Now all of it was reduced to ashes, swept away by the cruel hand of war.

Yet even amidst the overwhelming loss, Nancy clung fiercely to one thing. The love for her daughter, Marica. No matter the cost, no matter the danger, she would protect her with every fibre of her being. She was willing to sacrifice everything, even her own life, to keep her safe.

Singapore, 8th February 1942

The world was burning.

Marica took her first breath in a world already shattered by war. Born on February 14th as Singapore fell under siege, she entered a city consumed by fear. Once a thriving jewel of trade and culture, the place her parents had called home was now unrecognizable, held captive under the relentless grip of the Japanese Empire.

The streets, once vibrant with the voices of hawkers selling noodles and the clatter of busy feet, were now eerily silent. Only the distant rumble of explosions remained, along with the heavy thud of soldiers' boots echoing through the cracked roads and the anguished cries of those who had been taken, their fates swallowed by the darkness of war.

In the weeks leading up to the fall of Singapore, the city had been a powder keg of tension, with every alleyway and every street corner a potential battleground. The Japanese soldiers, in their crisp, khaki uniforms, moved in perfect formation, their rifles slung over their shoulders. Their uniforms were lightweight, designed for the humid tropics, with high-collared tunics and matching trousers tucked neatly into sturdy leather boots. Some wore steel helmets adorned with the Imperial Japanese Army emblem, while others had soft field caps with a cloth flap draping down their necks to shield them from the sweltering sun. Their belts were fastened tightly, holding pouches for ammunition and bayonets gleaming at their sides.

The soldiers moved like ghosts through the streets, their eyes cold and unyielding, their presence casting a darkness over Singapore that felt impossible to escape. There was no mercy in their gaze, no hesitation in their steps, only the relentless march of war swallowing everything in its path.

Nancy had seen things no woman should ever have to witness. She had watched helplessly as neighbours were dragged from their homes, their faces frozen in terror, their screams cutting through the night like shattered glass. She had heard the gunshots, the crackling of burning buildings, and the anguished cries of those who had lost everything.

And then, on a night when the world outside had already fallen apart, Nancy's own life became a fight for survival.

"The Japanese are coming!" Henry's voice sliced through the night, sharp and frantic, filled with a desperation that left no room for doubt. He was a young man, still carrying the remnants of boyhood in his features, but the war had aged him beyond his years. He burst into their small wooden shack, breath coming in ragged gasps, sweat dripping down his face.

Nancy instinctively drew Marica closer to her chest, her infant daughter swaddled tightly in the sarong. She had become injured to the overwhelming stench of smoke and burning flesh, but the gnawing fear in her gut, that hollow feeling of impending doom, never left.

"Where do we go?" Nancy whispered, her voice trembling in the suffocating tension. Her heart raced, thudding in her chest with a force that threatened to suffocate her.

Henry's face was ghostly white, a stark contrast to the chaos unfolding outside. "There's no safe place, Nancy. They've surrounded the kampong. We have to run."

The world beyond their door was ablaze. The crackling of flames reached their ears, a constant, menacing sound, mingled with the distant crack of gunfire. Nancy's hands shook as she held Marica close, the baby's soft breath offering a fragile comfort in the midst of all the madness.

With no time to waste, they fled, bursting through the back door, stumbling across the dirt roads that led to the dense jungle bordering the village. The night felt alive with the sounds of war, the dull thud of bombs falling in the distance, their explosions shaking the ground beneath their feet. The anguished cries of those who had not been fast enough to escape echoed behind them, but there was no time to look back.

"Keep running! Don't stop!" Henry's voice rang out, strained and barely above the chaos surrounding them, as he urged them on.

Nancy stumbled, her feet bare and bleeding from the rough ground, but she didn't stop. Every breath felt like it was tearing through her chest, but she held onto Marica, unwilling to let go. The fear of losing her daughter was greater than the pain in her body.

They ran for hours, their stomachs empty, their throats dry. The jungle offered them some refuge from the soldiers, but the danger was far from over. They could hear the soldiers searching the area, their boots crunching over the leaves, their voices harsh and guttural.

Nancy collapsed by a small creek, her body shaking from exhaustion. She hadn't stopped running since they'd fled the kampong, and the lack of food and water was beginning to take its toll. Henry dropped beside her, his breath ragged.

"Honey, I'm so thirsty..." Henry whispered, his voice barely audible. His lips were cracked, and his skin had taken on a dull pallor from dehydration.

Nancy looked at him helplessly, her heart aching. She had nothing left to offer. The last of the water they had brought with them was gone, and even little Marica, nestled in her arms, was beginning to stir restlessly.

Just as they began to lose hope, an old man, hunched with age and covered in grime, appeared from the shadows. He had the eyes of someone who had seen too much, but there was a quiet strength about him.

"You need to keep moving," he said, his voice gruff, but there was an urgency to it. "The Japanese are still hunting for people. You cannot stay here."

Nancy looked up at him, her eyes wide with desperation. "But where do we go? We can't run forever."

The old man paused, his eyes scanning the dense jungle with a keen alertness, as though weighing the trustworthiness of those before him. His skin, dark and weathered from countless days beneath the sun, bore the marks of a life lived in the harshness of the wild. A long, tangled white beard fell to his chest, and his hair, once dark, was now streaked with grey, framed by a weather-beaten face etched with deep lines.

His clothes, simple and threadbare, seemed to have been shaped by the land itself, blending seamlessly with the earth around him. In his hands, he held a gnarled staff, worn smooth from years of use, a tool as old and steadfast as the man himself. After a long silence, he gave a slow, deliberate nod. "Follow me," he said, his voice a rasp, steady and unwavering despite the uncertainty surrounding them.

He led them deeper into the jungle, where the dense trees and thick foliage offered some semblance of safety. They walked in silence, each step measured and careful. As they walked, Nancy's thoughts kept returning to Marica, her baby girl, still so small, still so fragile in this war-torn world.

After what felt like hours, they reached a small cave hidden beneath a grove of large trees. It wasn't much, but it was shelter. The old man gestured for them to enter, and they did so without hesitation. Inside, the air was thick with dampness, but it offered a reprieve from the dangers outside.

Days dragged on, each one stretching into the next, making time feel as if it had come to a standstill. Marica's cries were constant, weak sobs of hunger, her tiny body growing more fragile with every passing hour. Henry had stopped asking for water, his voice lost to the dryness in his throat. Nancy, though hallowed by her own hunger, focused all her energy on keeping Marica alive, though it felt like an impossible task. The gnawing emptiness in their bellies was a constant reminder of their desperation.

Survival meant relying on the jungle. They ate what little the land offered, ceri kampung, the wild cherry that grew in patches among the trees, belimbing hutan, the tart starfruit that grew in the damp corners of the forest, and buah kundang, marian plums that stained their fingers yellow. Roots, when they were lucky enough to find them, and rainwater collected in cupped hands became their only sustenance. The jungle, though rich with life, was not generous to those who were desperate, and each day without food or water was a test of their will. The fear of being discovered by the Japanese soldiers was never far from their minds, the threat hanging over them like a dark cloud.

One afternoon, as the oppressive heat of the jungle pressed down on them, Nancy and Henry heard the unmistakable sound of footsteps crunching on the dry leaves just outside their cave. The soldiers were close. Nancy's breath caught in her throat, and her heart pounded in her chest, the sound deafening in her ears. She turned to look at Henry, and the silent terror in his eyes reflected her own.

Henry's face was drawn, his features hard and grim. His hand clenched into a fist, as if holding onto something, anything, that could anchor him in the storm of fear that threatened to consume them both.

"What do we do?" Henry whispered, his voice trembling, the panic in his words impossible to disguise. It was a question no one wanted to ask, but the weight of the answer hung in the air between them like a death sentence.

Nancy's mind raced. The cave could not protect them much longer. "We have to leave. Quietly. Don't make a sound."

They huddled together, waiting in the darkness, their breaths shallow and quick. The soldiers passed by without noticing the cave. Nancy let out a breath she hadn't realized she'd been holding.

But there was no time to rest. The war had come to their doorstep, and they would have to keep running, keep hiding, until they found a place to call home once again.

As the days turned to weeks, Nancy, Henry, and Marica grew thinner, their faces gaunt, their spirits broken. But they kept moving, kept surviving, even as the war raged on around them.

The sounds of gunfire, the screams of the innocent, the roar of the bombers, it was all part of the new world they had been forced to live in. But amid the madness, Nancy held on to the only thing she had left: the fierce love for her daughter, the unspoken promise to protect her at all costs.

One night, under the cover of darkness, Nancy knew they had to make their escape. The cave had sheltered them for weeks, but they couldn't survive on wild fruits and rainwater forever. The war was closing in. If they stayed, they would be found.

Nancy whispered her plan to Henry. "We follow the river," she said. "It leads to the coast. If we can get there, maybe, just maybe, we can find a way out."

Chapter 2: A Refuge in Pulau Ubin

Henry nodded; his face grim but determined. He helped Marica onto Nancy's back, her small arms wrapping tightly around her mother's neck. Then, they stepped out of the cave and into the night, their bodies moving like shadows among the trees.

The jungle was thick, the undergrowth clawing at their legs as they moved carefully through the darkness. The air was heavy with the scent of damp earth and danger. In the distance, they heard the rumble of military trucks, the occasional burst of gunfire. But they didn't stop. They couldn't.

Hours turned into days. They walked only at night, resting in the heat of the day beneath thick foliage. Hunger gnawed at their bellies, exhaustion weighed on their limbs, but the thought of freedom pushed them forward.

Then, one evening, as the sun dipped below the horizon, they heard it, the gentle lapping of waves against the shore. They had made it to the coast.

Nancy's heart pounded. "We need a boat," she whispered to Henry.

They crept along the shoreline, their eyes scanning the darkness for any sign of help. Then, they saw it, a small wooden fishing boat tied to a post.

A lone fisherman stood nearby, his face weary but kind. Nancy didn't know if he would help them, but she had no choice. She stepped forward, cradling Marica in her arms.

"Please," she whispered. "We need to leave."

The fisherman studied them, his eyes filled with understanding. He had seen many families like theirs, desperate, clinging to hope. Without a word, he nodded and motioned for them to get in.

As the boat pushed off the shore, Nancy looked back at the land they were leaving behind. The land that had been her home. The land that had been ravaged by war.

Marica stirred in her arms, letting out a soft whimper. Nancy gently rocked her, pressing a kiss to her forehead. "Shh, my love," she whispered. "We're almost there."

As the boat drifted into the vast unknown, Nancy knew the war had not won. They had survived. And as long as they had each other, there was hope.

The boat rocked gently on the dark waves as they drifted further from the shore. Nancy held Marica close, wrapping her in the thin shawl she had carried since they fled their home. Henry sat beside them, his eyes fixed on the horizon, scanning for danger. The fisherman, a quiet man with deep lines etched into his face, rowed steadily, his muscles tensing with each pull of the oars.

"Where are you taking us?" Nancy finally asked, her voice barely above a whisper.

"To a nearby island," the fisherman said, his voice rough but reassuring. "Pulau Ubin. The Japanese don't patrol there much. You'll be safe for now."

Nancy felt a wave of relief wash over her. Pulau Ubin. A small, quiet island off Singapore's coast, untouched by the horrors of war. It wasn't the freedom she longed for, but it was a flicker of hope, a place to rest, even if only for a while.

As the first rays of sunlight touched the water, painting the sky in soft shades of pink and gold, the island came into view. The thick jungle ahead stood tall and proud, a stark contrast to the shattered world they had left behind. The only sounds now were the gentle chirping of birds, the distant cries of the jungle, and the steady hum of the boat cutting through the water.

The fisherman steered the boat toward a small jetty. "There's a village deeper inland," he said. "Find an old woman named Ah Ma. She helps those who need to disappear."

Nancy's chest tightened with gratitude, a mix of hope and exhaustion pooling in her heart. "Thank you," she whispered, pressing her hands together in a quiet gesture of thanks.

The fisherman nodded, his weathered face calm yet kind, before pushing off into the water, disappearing into the horizon as quietly as he had arrived.

Henry helped Nancy and Marica off the boat, the rough wood of the jetty under their feet feeling like a blessing after days adrift on the water.

As their feet touched solid ground, a moment of peace washed over them. They were here. Safe, for now.

With Marica still clinging to her, Nancy led the way into the jungle. Her bare feet sank into the soft earth, the coolness of the ground a reminder that they were no longer running. The air smelled of damp leaves and earthy moss, the scent of the forest enveloping them as they moved forward.

They walked in silence, the hours stretching on, the weight of their journey pressing down on them. Then, in the distance, a plume of smoke rose into the sky, a sign of life, of hope. They quickened their pace, drawn toward it like a beacon.

Nancy's heart raced, but this time, it was not from fear. It was the hope that they were about to find something, someone, that could help them begin anew.

A cluster of wooden huts appeared, hidden among the trees. Chickens clucked in the dirt, and villagers carried baskets filled with fruits and fish. Life here moved at a different pace, quiet, untouched.

Nancy hesitated before approaching a small hut where an old woman sat on a wooden stool, peeling mangosteens with steady hands.

Ah Ma was an older woman with a face weathered by time, her skin deeply lined and tanned from years spent under the sun. Her hair, silver and thinning, was tied back in a loose knot, and her eyes, sharp and observant, seemed to see through the veil of fear that clung to Nancy and her family. She wore a simple tunic, faded from wear, and her hands, though wrinkled, moved with the steady grace of someone accustomed to caring for others. Her presence was calm but firm, a quiet strength emanating from her like the roots of an ancient tree.

"You are looking for Ah Ma," she said before Nancy could speak, her voice low but steady. Her keen gaze flicked over them. "You are running. I am Ah Ma."

Nancy swallowed hard, her throat dry, and nodded. "Please. We need help."

Ah Ma let out a slow sigh, as if weighing the situation, before stepping aside and gesturing for them to follow her into the hut. The inside was humble, with wooden floors worn smooth by time, a simple straw mat on the ground, and the lingering scent of herbal medicine filling the air. It was a sanctuary of sorts, a place of refuge amidst the chaos outside.

"You may stay here for now," Ah Ma said, handing Nancy a bowl of rice. "But the war is long. If you truly wish to be free, you must leave Singapore."

Nancy's grip tightened around the bowl. Leave Singapore. The thought sent fear and longing crashing over her. But she knew Ah Ma was right. They could not stay in hiding forever.

Henry looked at Nancy, determination in his tired eyes. "We need to find a way to Malaya," he said.

Nancy nodded, pressing a kiss to Marica's hair. She didn't know how they would do it, but one thing was certain.

They had come too far to stop now.

As the days passed in Pulau Ubin, Nancy, Henry, and Marica slowly began to adapt to their new life. The village, though quiet and peaceful, was a stark contrast to the horrors of war they had left behind. The gentle hum of daily life, the sound of roosters crowing at dawn, the rustling of leaves in the tropical breeze, and the laughter of children playing near the river was a balm to their weary souls.

Ah Ma, the village elder, proved to be a source of strength and wisdom. She showed Nancy how to forage for edible plants and taught her how to fish using simple bamboo rods. The villagers, though wary of strangers at first, accepted Nancy and her family with quiet hospitality. They offered what little they had, coconuts, fresh fish, and wild fruits. They didn't ask questions, and Nancy didn't volunteer answers. In this place, silence was as valuable as food.

Marica, though still thin and fragile, found joy in the simplicity of island life. She spent her days playing with the other village children, collecting seashells along the shore, or watching the fishermen cast their nets into the sea. Henry, too, found solace in the rhythm of the island, spending his time helping the men build new huts, repair boats, or tend to the small vegetable patches scattered across the village.

But even in this quiet sanctuary, the shadows of the war still loomed.

At night, Nancy could hear the distant rumble of bombers far off in the sky. The occasional whisper of a passing plane would send a chill through her, but she had learned to ignore it, to focus instead on the present moment.

One evening, as the sun dipped below the horizon and painted the sky in shades of purple and orange, Nancy sat on the edge of the village, looking out at the vast expanse of the South China Sea. The waves lapped gently against the shore, a stark reminder of the peace they had found here, far from the destruction of war.

Henry joined her, sitting down quietly beside her. For a moment, they just watched the sunset, the beauty of the moment too overwhelming to put into words.

"Do you think we'll ever be able to go back?" Nancy asked, her voice soft as she watched the last rays of light fade into the night.

Henry shook his head. "I don't know. But for now, this is our home. We've made it this far, haven't we?"

Nancy nodded, her heart heavy with a mixture of gratitude and sorrow. The war had stolen so much from them, but it hadn't stolen their will to survive. Here, on this small island, they had found a temporary haven. But as she looked out at the sea, Nancy knew that someday, they would have to move on again. The war was still out there, and it would not be forgotten.

For now, though, they were safe. And for now, that was enough.

Life in Pulau Ubin offered Nancy, Henry, and Marica a strange peace amid the chaos of the world around them. Though it was far removed from the modernity of Singapore, the island was rich in its own way, lush, quiet, and self-sustaining. The villagers lived simply, growing their own food, fishing in the nearby waters, and relying on the land for their daily needs. The sounds of nature replaced the noise of the city, and Nancy found comfort in the rhythm of island life.

Every morning, Nancy would wake with the first light, the soft murmur of the sea, a constant presence in the background. She started the day by gathering water from a nearby well, and Henry would go off to work with the village men, repairing boats or building structures. Over time, he became an essential part of the community, teaching the villagers skills they didn't have and learning from them in return.

For Marica, the island was a playground. She grew stronger every day, her cheeks gaining colour as she played with the other children, climbing trees, running barefoot through the dirt, and swimming in the shallow waters of the sea. She loved the wildness of Pulau Ubin, the freedom it offered. Sometimes she would run to the forest to collect berries or watch the fishermen haul in their catch, their boats creaking under the weight of the day's bounty.

Nancy spent many afternoons with the older villagers, listening to their stories about life on the island. They spoke of simpler times, of a world before the war, and shared tales of the jungle and the creatures that lived in its depths.

She learned how to weave palm fronds into baskets, how to prepare local herbs for medicine, and how to catch fish with nothing but a piece of twine. These moments filled her with a sense of purpose, something she had lost when the war began.

But no matter how much the island became their sanctuary, the shadow of the war was never far. Every now and then, they would hear whispers about the war's progression, rumours that the Japanese forces were retreating, and that the Allies were gaining ground. Nancy would sit with Henry in the evenings, as they both tried to grasp the reality of what this might mean for their future.

The war ended in 1945, marking a turning point in Nancy, Henry, and Marica's journey. As the year progressed, they heard the news that the Japanese forces had surrendered, and the war was finally over. This momentous event brought a mixture of relief and disbelief to those who had endured the horrors of conflict.

Three years had passed since they had sought refuge in Pulau Ubin. Marica, who had been a baby when they first arrived on the island, was now three years old. Her small frame carried the innocence of a child who had known nothing but the jungle and the makeshift shelter they called home. Though they had found safety in the quiet isolation of Pulau Ubin, the longing for their home in Singapore had never fully faded.

As the war came to an end, Henry found himself facing a different battle. Though he had brought his family to safety, his duty was far from over. A former air force officer, he was called back to Singapore to help rebuild the country, to protect what remained of a nation still reeling from destruction. His sense of duty ran deep, stronger than ever.

One evening, after a quiet dinner beneath the soft glow of lantern light, Henry reached for Nancy's hand, his grip firm but filled with unspoken sorrow. "I have to go back," he said, his voice steady, though laced with the weight of the decision. "Singapore needs me. I have to help rebuild. I have to do my part."

Nancy's heart clenched. She had fought so hard to keep their family together, to keep him safe. Her eyes shimmered with both pride and fear. "Henry, we've come so far," she whispered. "Please, don't leave us now."

He lifted a hand to her cheek, his touch lingering. "It's the only way forward, Nancy. We have to be strong. For Marica. For ourselves."

As dawn painted the sky in soft hues of gold and rose, Henry gathered what little he had and bid farewell to Nancy and Marica. The island that had sheltered them now became a place of parting. He turned one last time before disappearing into the jungle, the weight of uncertainty pressing upon them all.

For Nancy, life on Pulau Ubin became one of quiet resilience. Alone, she bore the responsibility of raising Marica, of creating something stable in a world still trembling from the aftershocks of war. Yet, through the loneliness, she clung to hope, hope that Henry would return, hope that the life they had fought so hard to protect would one day be whole again.

Though distance separated them, they remained bound by love, by sacrifice, by the unwavering belief that better days lay ahead. And just as the tide always found its way back to shore, Nancy believed that, in time, Henry would find his way back to them.

Chapter 3: Echoes of Love: A Final Goodbye (1945)

One afternoon, as the sun dipped low over the water, the villagers gathered at the shoreline, their eyes fixed on the small boat cutting through the waves. It carried a group of Allied soldiers, their faces weary, their uniforms dirtied by war, but there was something in their eyes, a flicker of hope. They were the first sign that everything was about to change.

The soldiers spoke of the Japanese surrender, of the empire's collapse, of peace returning to the land after years of fear and suffering. The words spread through the island like wildfire, whispered from one villager to the next. And for the first time in what felt like a lifetime, Nancy let herself believe. It was over. The war was finally over.

But as the boat drifted closer, a feeling of unease settled deep in Nancy's chest. There was something else. Something she wasn't ready for.

Her breath caught as her gaze landed on a small bundle cradled in the arms of one of the soldiers, wrapped carefully in a tattered blanket. Her heart pounded. A terrible feeling filled her before anyone could say the words.

It was Henry.

Nancy's knees nearly buckled. The world tilted, and she gripped the wooden beams of the dock to steady herself. She wanted to run, to scream, to make it not true. But there he was, his face pale, his body still. The man who had been her anchor, who had carried them through the darkest nights, was gone.

The war had stolen him from her.

Nancy's hands trembled as she held the worn notebook, her vision blurring with tears. The weight of it in her grasp was almost too much to bear. Henry's. The last piece of him.

She took a shaky breath and opened it, her fingers tracing the ink-stained pages. His words were there, written in his familiar hand, strong, deliberate, but smudged in places, as if he had been fighting against time itself to write them. Her chest ached as she turned to the final page. And then, she saw it.

My beloved Nancy,

If you're reading this, then I may not be coming home. I've tried to push the thought away, to tell myself that I will see you and Marica again, but war has a way of stealing certainty. As I sit here, listening to the echoes of battle, I can't shake the feeling that the odds are against me.

But through it all, you and Marica have been my light, my reason to keep fighting. Every time exhaustion threatened to pull me under, every time fear whispered that I would not survive the night, I thought of you, your laughter, the way your eyes shine when you smile, the warmth of your hand in mine. I have held onto those memories like a man drowning, reaching for the only thing that keeps him afloat.

I wanted to be there for Marica's first heartbreak, her first job, to walk her down the aisle one day.

I wanted to be there to hold your hand, to grow old with you, to sit on the porch and watch the world slow down around us. That was the life I dreamed of. That was the future I fought for.

But dreams don't always survive war.

I don't know what the next moment holds, but I do know this, you and Marica were my greatest love, my greatest joy. Every step I took on this battlefield, I took for you. I fought so that one day, you could wake up without fear, so that our daughter could grow up in a world where peace was more than just a distant hope.

If I don't make it home, please don't let my love become a ghost that haunts you. Let it be something that lifts you, that reminds you of all the moments we had, rather than the ones we lost. Tell Marica that I love her, that I will always be with her, watching over her in the quiet moments, in the stars that light up the night sky.

And Nancy, my love, know that if there is anything beyond this life, I will find my way back to you. Always.

Forever yours,
Henry

Nancy pressed the pages to her chest, as if holding them close might somehow bring him back. But Henry was gone. The war had taken him. And yet, as she stood there beneath the open sky, with Marica's small fingers wrapped tightly around her own, she felt it, his love, unbroken, unwavering.

Somewhere in the distance, the sun was rising. Nancy's heart seemed to stop. Henry had known. He had known he might not return, yet he had clung to the hope that somehow, they would be together again. His words were the last gift he could give her a gift of love, hope, and an unspoken goodbye.

Tears streamed down her face as she clutched the notebook to her chest. The pain of losing him was unbearable. She would never again hear his voice, never again feel the warmth of his embrace. The war had taken him just as peace had seemed within reach.

As she stood at the edge of the dock, she watched the boat carrying Henry's body disappear down the river, bound for the small village where he would be laid to rest. A storm of emotions churned inside her. She wanted to run, to escape the grief threatening to consume her, but she knew she couldn't. She had to carry on for herself, for Marica, and for Henry's memory. His love would always be with her.

"I love you, Henry. Always," she whispered into the wind.

That night, unable to bear the weight of her sorrow, Nancy ran. She didn't know where she was going, only that she had to move, to escape the walls closing in around her. Barefoot, she stumbled into the jungle, the damp earth cool beneath her feet. The thick mist curled around her, wrapping her in silence. Her breaths came in ragged sobs as she fell to her knees, her body shaking.

"I don't know how to do this," she whispered. "I don't know how to go on without you."

Then, something shifted. A presence, familiar, steady.

Nancy hesitated, barely daring to look up. But when she did, her breath caught. A figure stood ahead, tall, strong, impossibly real.

"Henry?" her voice trembled.

The mist swirled, but he remained, his presence unmistakable. A jolt of pain surged through her chest. Was this real? Or was her grief playing cruel tricks on her?

Tears welled in her eyes as she reached out. "Please, Henry. I can't do this without you. I don't know how to breathe without you."

Silence. And then, his voice, soft as the wind, steady as the tide.

"Nancy…"

A sob tore from her lips. "Is it really you?"

"I'm here. I've never left you."

She reached for him, but her hands met only empty air. A fresh wave of grief washed over her.

"I don't know how to keep going," she choked out. "It hurts so much."

Henry's voice surrounded her, warm and familiar. "You carry on, Nancy. For me. For Marica. You are stronger than you know."

She shook her head. "I'm not."

"Yes, you are," he whispered. "You've always been strong. And you're not alone. I am with you, always. In every step you take, in every moment of peace."

Nancy closed her eyes, letting his words settle deep in her soul. The ache of loss would never truly leave her, but Henry's love had not disappeared. It was woven into her very being.

With a steadying breath, she whispered, "I will. For you. For Marica."

The mist began to lift, and as it did, Henry's figure faded. But his presence remained, no longer a ghost of sorrow but a quiet strength within her.

She wasn't alone.

She would keep going.

Chapter 4: A Life Reborn from the Ashes

After the war, when the world seemed to stop spinning and the dust began to settle, Nancy was left to pick up the shattered pieces of a life that had been irrevocably changed. The loss of her husband, the man who had been her partner, her anchor, and the father of their child, left a void so deep and raw that at times, she wondered if she would ever feel whole again.

But in the silence of her grief, there was a quiet, persistent force, the love for her daughter, Marica. The tiny hands that clung to her, the innocent eyes that searched hers for comfort, became the reason Nancy couldn't give up. In those early days, when the war's horrors still clung to her mind like a dark cloud, Nancy could only focus on one thing: survival.

The life she had once known was gone, stolen by the ravages of war. The familiar sounds of laughter and joy had been replaced by the eerie stillness of a world trying to rebuild itself. It felt as if the war had taken everything from her, the life she had envisioned with her husband, the future she had dreamed of for her daughter, the peace she had longed for.

Yet, despite the overwhelming grief, Nancy did not falter. She couldn't. For Marica. For the memory of her husband, and for herself.

In the weeks that followed, she worked tirelessly, doing whatever she could to keep a roof over their heads and food on the table.

The world around them seemed to slowly awaken from its nightmare, but for Nancy, the pain of loss lingered in every corner of their small, cramped home. The faint scent of her husband's cologne still lingered in the clothes she couldn't bring herself to pack away, and his absence echoed through every room, every quiet moment.

Nancy's strength came from the unspoken promise she had made to Henry before he left to protect Marica and ensure she had a future, no matter what. In the months that followed, she worked tirelessly, rising with the sun to tend to the crops in the village, her hands rough from pulling weeds and harvesting fruit. When the tides were right, she waded into the shallow waters with the other women, collecting clams and fish to trade for supplies. The days were long, her body ached from the labour, but it was a small price to pay for the future she was fighting for a future where Marica could grow up without fear, without the shadow of war looming over her.

Though she had no family nearby, no close friends to lean on, Nancy found solace in the small moments with Marica. There were no grand gestures, no sweeping romantic moments to lift her spirit. But in the quiet, tender moments when Marica would fall asleep in her arms, or when she would bring home a drawing she'd made, scrawled with childish pride Nancy found the strength to carry on.

But it wasn't just for Marica. Nancy, too, had dreams, dreams that had been silenced by the brutal reality of the war but were now beginning to stir once again.

She had once been a woman who had hoped for a life of happiness and love, a life of partnership with the man she had loved. Now, in the quiet of her grief, she began to dream of a new life, a life where she could stand on her own, a life where she could give Marica everything she needed to thrive.

But that was not to say the road was easy. Nancy's days were long and tiring, and the weight of responsibility rested heavily on her shoulders. She often found herself exhausted, both mentally and physically, struggling to balance the demands of work and motherhood, longing for the days when the weight of the world hadn't been so overwhelming.

Yet even in the darkest moments, Nancy held fast to the belief that she was capable of rebuilding their lives. She wasn't sure how, and she wasn't sure when, but she knew that she couldn't let the past define them. She would honour her husband's memory by living fully by fighting for a future where Marica could flourish.

As Marica grew, Nancy began to see glimpses of the woman her daughter would become. The determination, the spark of hope that had once burned in Nancy's heart now shone in her daughter's eyes. Marica may have lost her father before she could truly know him, but she had inherited his strength and resilience, and Nancy could see it in every word she spoke, every step she took.

It was these small victories, these moments of quiet progress, which helped Nancy hold on to the belief that life would be better, that they could heal from the scars the war had left behind.

There were still days when the grief felt too heavy to bear, when the longing for the life they had lost threatened to pull them under. But those days were fewer now, and Nancy had learned to embrace the hope that had once seemed so out of reach.

In the years that followed, Nancy built a life that, while far from perfect, was theirs. It was a life filled with hard work, laughter, and love. A life that Marica would one day look back on and understand was built on the strength of a mother's love, the memory of a man who had given everything for their future, and the resilience to rise from the ashes of war.

And as they moved forward, Nancy knew that her husband's spirit would always be with them, not just in the memories of what they had lost, but in the future they were now building together.

As the evening light dimmed, Marica sat on the floor, gripping a crayon in her small hand. Her drawing was a swirl of colours, mostly wobbly shapes and lines but to her, it was something special. She looked up at Nancy with wide, curious eyes.

"Is this what Daddy looked like?" she asked, holding up her picture.

Nancy's heart ached at the question. Marica had been too young to truly remember Henry, but she knew him through the stories Nancy told, the faded photographs she traced with her tiny fingers, and the way her mother spoke about him with love.

Nancy smiled gently, pulling Marica into her lap. "That's beautiful, sweetheart. Daddy would love it."

Marica snuggled against her, resting her head on Nancy's chest. "Do you think he can see it?"

Nancy kissed the top of her head and whispered, "I think he sees everything, my love. And I know he's so proud of you."

Marica yawned, her small arms wrapping around her mother. "Will you tell me a story about Daddy again?"

"Of course," Nancy said, rocking her gently. "Let me tell you about the time he carried you on his shoulders, and you laughed so hard the whole village could hear…"

As Nancy spoke, the weight of grief lifted, if only for a moment. Henry may have been gone, but his love lived on in their stories, in Marica's innocent questions, and in the quiet strength that kept them moving forward.

Chapter 5: A Girl in a Changing World

The air was thick with dust and the scent of construction as Marica stood on the edge of the bustling city, her grown hands gripping the smooth steel fence that now marked the boundary of what had once been their home. Singapore, a place that had known nothing but the scars of war, had risen from the ashes. The streets, once cracked and burned, now stretched wide and smooth, lined with tall, gleaming buildings reaching toward the sky.

The old black-and-white colonial houses, once standing proudly but now broken and forgotten, had been replaced with modern apartments, commercial hubs, and clean boulevards. The city, now alive with progress, stood as a symbol of resilience, a testament to its ability to rebuild itself. For Marica, however, the transformation of Singapore was bittersweet. The war had taken so much, but it had also shaped her into the woman she had become. Yet, despite the changes, part of her still carried the weight of the past.

Fifteen years had passed since her father, Henry, had died here in Singapore. Henry had been a man of integrity, hardworking and kind, but in the chaos of those turbulent times, even the strongest had been swept away. His death had marked the end of an era for their family, leaving her mother, Nancy, to pick up the pieces. The loss of her father, the man who had been the cornerstone of their world, was a wound that time had failed to heal. Still, Marica had learned to live without him, carrying his memory as a silent, constant presence in her heart.

Her mother, Nancy, had never spoken much about Henry after his death. The pain was too raw, too deep. It was easier for her to pretend he had simply vanished, like so many others in those days. Instead, she focused on the task of raising her child, Marica, just a little girl when her father was gone.

Those years had been the hardest for Nancy, but she never wavered. She worked tirelessly, day and night, to keep their small family together, ensuring Marica had food to eat and clothes to wear. As the world around them rebuilt, so did Nancy, determined to secure a future for her daughter.

Now, as 1960 arrived, Singapore was no longer the war-torn city it had once been. The scars of war had faded, replaced by a city eager to redefine itself. Shophouses, once worn and crumbling, bustled with life as small businesses thrived. The once crowded slums and kampongs slowly gave way to modern housing estates, as the government introduced new high-rise flats to accommodate the growing population. The streets, once dusty and filled with rickshaws, now saw the rise of buses and motorcars, symbols of a rapidly changing world.

Factories and industries began to take root, with manufacturing sectors such as textiles, electronics, and shipbuilding emerging across the city. These new industries created jobs and opportunities for families like theirs, shifting Singapore's economy from trade based to manufacturing driven.

The streets remained alive with the rich aroma of hawker food as vendors served steaming bowls of noodles, sizzling skewers of satay, and fragrant curries. The air buzzed with a symphony of languages, English, Malay, Mandarin, and Tamil, a reflection of the diverse cultures coexisting in a nation forging its identity.

Yet, despite the modern changes, the past still lingered, a quiet reminder to Nancy of all they had lost.

Marica was no longer the scared little girl clinging to her mother's side in the midst of chaos. She had grown into a young woman of 18, her heart now filled with the quiet confidence that came from surviving and rebuilding. She sat now at the same small wooden table that had once been their only space for eating and studying, watching her mother as she worked the old sewing machine, the rhythmic sound filling the room. The house, though modest, was far different from the dilapidated shanty town they had once called home. The neighbourhood had transformed along with the city, but Marica knew it was her mother's relentless strength that had brought them here.

"Marica," Nancy said, pausing in her work, wiping a bead of sweat from her brow. "You're 18 now. You've seen the world change, and now it's time to think about your future. Have you thought about what you want to do?"

Marica's heartbeat faster at the question. She had been waiting for this moment. This crossroad where she would step into the future, ready to take her place in the world.

She had always known she would have to leave the small world her mother had created for her, but she hadn't expected it to feel so big, so real, in this moment.

"I have been thinking about it, Mama," Marica said, her voice steady, though her hands trembled slightly. "I have been offered a job at Changi Airport, a junior clerk position. It is a good start, and they are even providing a small one bedroom apartment nearby. It would help us. It could be a way forward."

Nancy set the sewing machine aside, her hands trembling as she reached for Marica's. Her tired eyes filled with pride and joy.

"Oh, my girl," Nancy said, her voice brimming with emotion. "You have always wanted more and now it is happening. I have worked my whole life to give you the chance to build something better, something beyond what I had. And look at you now. You are making it happen."

Tears pricked Marica's eyes as warmth spread through her chest. "But Mama," she said softly, her voice catching. "I do not want to leave you. You have always been my strength. What will you do without me?"

Nancy squeezed her hands gently, smiling through her own tears. "You do not need to worry about me, my dear. Knowing you are safe, independent and building your future makes me the happiest mother in the world. This is what I have prayed for. And your apartment, it will be your own little home, close enough to visit whenever you want."

Marica swallowed the lump in her throat. "I promise, Mama. I will never forget where I come from. I will make you proud."

Nancy pulled her daughter into a tight embrace, her heart swelling with happiness. The sound of the sewing machine, the distant hum of the city, all faded as Marica held onto her mother, feeling the bittersweet mix of past and future.

The city had changed and so had she. It was time to take the next step, to carve out her own path. The past would always be with her, but the future was waiting, and she was ready.

Chapter 6: A New Beginning

Marica's first day at Changi Airport felt like stepping into another world. The vast terminal stretched endlessly before her, alive with the hum of activity, travellers rushing to catch their flights, the soft click of high heels on the polished floors, and the steady hum of flight announcements filling the air. The smells of freshly brewed coffee, sweet perfume, and the faint tang of jet fuel mixed together in a heady cocktail that spoke of possibilities and far off places. Everything was so new, so clean, so organized. Nothing like the dusty alleyways of her old neighbourhood or the crumbling shantytown where survival had been a daily struggle.

The airport was bustling with energy, and yet there was an order to it that Marica had never known before. The staff moved with precision, dressed in navy blue uniforms with gold trim, their faces set in professional expressions. They knew their place, their purpose. And Marica? She wasn't sure where she fit in yet, but she was determined to find out. She had spent her entire life fighting just to get by; now, this place felt like a stepping stone toward something bigger, something that had the potential to change everything for her.

Her first task was simple, sorting through piles of paperwork, filing documents, answering phone calls, and managing schedules. The work was mundane, yes, but even in the simplest tasks, Marica found a deep sense of purpose. The noise of the airport faded into the background as she focused, immersing herself in the work. The steady rhythm of her tasks felt like a small victory.

She was no longer just surviving; she was contributing, building something for herself.

Each day, as the hours passed, Marica began to see the invisible threads that connected the airport to the wider world, connections to countries she had only ever dreamed of, connections to people who were chasing their own dreams. And for the first time in a long while, she felt a spark of possibility within her. It was as though she had stumbled upon the edge of something grand.

One afternoon, as she sat at her desk organising the flight schedules, a voice interrupted her thoughts.

"You're new here, aren't you?" The voice was cheerful, warm with a touch of curiosity.

Marica looked up to see a young woman standing at her desk, her dark, wavy hair bouncing with each step. She wore the standard airport uniform, a navy blue blouse with gold trim, and her name tag read *Lina*. There was an openness in Lina's smile that made Marica feel immediately at ease.

"Yes," Marica replied, a little shyly. "I just started last week."

Lina's smile widened, and she leaned against the desk casually. "Well, welcome to the madness of Changi," she said with a light laugh. "It's a good place to work, but you'll get used to the pace. It's all about learning on the job and helping each other out. You'll make friends in no time, trust me."

The words lingered in Marica's mind long after Lina walked away, a warm glow spreading through her chest. *Friends*, it had been a long time since she had allowed herself to think of friendship as something possible. She had always been so focused on survival, on taking care of her mother and herself. But here, in this whirlwind of motion and fresh faces, there was the chance for something different. Something better.

The days at Changi Airport began to blend together in a blur of motion. There were long hours spent behind a desk, phone calls that went on longer than expected, and moments where Marica felt overwhelmed by the noise and bustle. But with each passing day, she found herself growing more confident. The work was no longer just about completing tasks, it was about learning, adapting, and proving to herself that she could thrive in a world that was always changing.

As Marica sat at the kitchen table, the warm steam from her tea rising into the quiet evening, she gazed out the window, lost in the lights of the city below. There was a soft hum of life outside, a world that seemed to be waiting for her. After another long day at the airport, she felt as if she were on the cusp of something more, something beyond the struggle.

Her mother, Nancy, entered the room, her tired hands showing the toll of the day's work, yet her eyes were full of quiet love and patience. She sat down beside Marica, her voice gentle but filled with a knowing care. "How was your day, Marica?"

Marica's heart swelled with a new kind of hope, the kind she hadn't dared to let herself feel in years. She turned to her mother, her voice steady but full of emotion. "Mama, I think I'm finally getting there. Changi... it's everything I dreamed it would be and more. There's so much waiting for me. I want to give you the life you've always deserved. I want us to have everything we never had."

Nancy's eyes softened, and a single tear glistened in the corner of her eye as she reached across the table, taking Marica's hands in her own. The years of sacrifice were written in the lines of her skin, but in that simple touch, Marica felt the depth of her mother's love. "You already have, Marica," she whispered, her voice thick with gratitude and quiet pride.

Chapter 7: A Stranger with Blue Eyes

The 1960s arrived like a breath of fresh air in Singapore, filling the streets with a new energy, a sense of possibility that seemed to echo through every corner of the city. Young people, full of dreams and restless ambition, carried their transistor radios as they walked, the sound of The Beatles and The Rolling Stones spilling into the air like anthems of a generation. In the dimly lit dance halls, couples swayed to the fast, infectious rhythm of twist music, their hearts beating in time with the wild, carefree melodies. Even local bands like The Quests found their place in this musical revolution, proving that Singapore's soul could sing just as loudly as any Western city.

The fashion, too, was a reflection of this bold new world. Women traded in the conservative styles of the past for mini skirts, bright-coloured go-go boots, and daring PVC dresses that shimmered with every step. Their hair, often styled in soft curls or extravagant bouffant, framed their faces with a kind of carefree elegance, and bold eyeliner became the signature of a generation daring to redefine what it meant to be beautiful. The world seemed to be unfolding in front of Marica, and it was in the midst of this vibrant, whirlwind time that she would meet Edward. It would be a love that felt as timeless and unforgettable as the music playing in the background.

It was another ordinary day at Changi Airport, a place where countless lives intersected for just a brief moment, before drifting apart, never to cross again. The crowds moved in a steady flow, each person caught in their own world, unaware of the connections made and lost in the blink of an eye. Yet, Marica couldn't help but feel that there was more to these fleeting encounters than met the eye. Somewhere within the hustle and bustle, she would soon realize that sometimes, the briefest of moments can leave a lasting mark on a life, altering its course in ways she could never have imagined.

Marica moved through the crowded terminal of Changi Airport with a grace that seemed almost effortless, her uniform crisp, her hair softly curling around her face. A-line dresses and white go-go boots, the signature fashion of the time, suited her perfectly elegant yet approachable, professional yet undeniably feminine. She walked through the ebb and flow of travellers, a part of this world yet somehow set apart from it, like a dream that hadn't quite settled into reality.

As the loudspeaker crackled to life, the familiar strains of "I Want to Hold Your Hand" by The Beatles filled the air, drifting through the noise and the chaos. She found herself humming along, almost unconsciously, adjusting the delicate collar of her dress as the tune seemed to follow her every step. It played everywhere lately, on the radios of hawker stalls, in the dance halls where couples twisted and jived, and now here, in the airport where people said both hellos and goodbyes, as fleeting as the passing moments of their lives.

But then, in the middle of the constant motion, something or rather, someone stopped her.

He appeared out of the crowd, tall and effortlessly poised, his every movement exuding the kind of quiet confidence that could only come from a life lived in places far beyond her own. His Royal Air Force uniform was impeccably pressed, the insignia a badge of honour, and his golden blonde hair caught the light in a way that made him stand out against the sea of dark-haired travellers. But it wasn't just his appearance that captivated her, it was his eyes. The shade of blue so piercing, so intense, it felt as though the world stopped spinning for just a heartbeat.

For a moment that stretched beyond time, he looked at her.

Not a passing glance or a casual nod, but a gaze that lingered, steady and searching, as though he, too, felt the stir of something unspoken between them. The connection was instant, undeniable.

Marica's fingers curled slightly, her heart stuttered, and for a split second, it was as if the rest of the world disappeared, leaving only the two of them standing there, suspended in an unspoken understanding. It wasn't just that he was handsome, though he most certainly was, it was the way he looked at her, as though she was a puzzle he wanted to solve, a story he wanted to hear.

She should have looked away. She should have returned to her duties, to the quiet rhythm of her job.

She should have let him slip from her thoughts as quickly as he'd appeared. But for those few seconds, she didn't. She couldn't. The connection was too powerful, too real.

And then, just as quickly as he had come into her world, he was gone. He melted into the crowd, his uniform blending with the sea of people, and Marica was left standing there, her breath still caught in her chest.

Who was he?

She turned, searching the terminal with a sense of desperation, but he was already lost among the hundreds of faces, his presence nothing more than a fleeting memory.

49

Her chest rose and fell, her mind racing to make sense of what had just happened. She forced herself to take a steadying breath, to focus on the duties that lay ahead, to dismiss the strange connection as a brief moment in time, something that would be forgotten as soon as the next flight boarded.

But deep down, she knew better.

Some moments were destined to be forgotten. Others… were the beginning of something far greater than either person could imagine.

And though she had no way of knowing it then, that brief moment, that single glance, was about to change everything. Forever.

Chapter 8: A Twist of Fate at Sentosa Beach

The sun hung low in the sky, casting golden hues across the waves as the tide lapped at the shore. Sentosa Beach was alive with laughter, children building sandcastles, couples strolling along the water's edge, music drifting from a transistor radio nearby.

Marica sat on her beach towel, a paperback novel open in her lap, though she had long since stopped reading. She was enjoying the rare quiet, the salty breeze a welcome change from the air-conditioned chill of the airport.

Then, a shadow fell over her.

"Excuse me… but do I know you?"

She looked up and her breath caught.

Him.

The British Royal Air Force officer from Changi Airport.

Up close, he was even more striking. Gone was the stiff military uniform; in its place, a simple white shirt with the sleeves rolled up, khaki trousers that hinted at an athletic frame. His blonde hair was slightly tousled from the wind, his sharp features softened by the glow of the setting sun.

She stared for a second too long before finding her voice.

"I work at Changi Airport," she said finally. "I think we crossed paths there."

His lips curled into a half-smile, amused yet intrigued.

"Ah," he said. "That explains it." He extended his hand. "Edward Taylor."

She hesitated, then took it. His grip was warm, steady.

"Marica," she replied.

"Marica," he repeated, as though tasting the name. "A beautiful name for a beautiful woman."

She raised an eyebrow. "Do you say that to every woman you meet?"

He chuckled, utterly unfazed. "No, but I might start, just for you."

Despite herself, she smiled.

He glanced at the book in her lap. "What are you reading?"

She tilted the cover toward him. *Pride and Prejudice.*

"Ah, Jane Austen," he mused. "Let me guess, you're waiting for a Mr. Darcy to sweep you off your feet?"

Marica smirked. "And you think you fit the role?"

Edward placed a hand over his heart. "I'd like to think I have a bit more charm than Darcy."

She laughed, a real, unguarded laugh. Something about him put her at ease.

"Would it be too forward of me to ask if I could join you?" he asked.

Marica pretended to consider. "That depends. Are you going to bore me with Air Force stories?"

"I'll have you know, my stories are quite thrilling."

"In that case," she said, scooting over, "have a seat, Airman."

And just like that, conversation flowed effortlessly between them, like they had known each other far longer than a handful of fleeting moments. They talked for hours, their words weaving between laughter and stories, as the sky melted from blue to amber, then into the dusky hues of twilight. It was only when the beach began to empty, when the tide crept closer to their feet, that they realized how much time had passed. Edward hesitated, as if reluctant to let the evening slip away completely. Then, with quiet certainty, he asked, "Can I see you again?"

And she had said yes.

For the first time in a long while, Marica felt something shift deep inside her.

Fate, it seemed, had been waiting for this very moment.

From that night on, they were inseparable.

The next day they met for late night movies at the Capitol Theatre, where the scent of buttered popcorn lingered in the air and the flickering light of the screen cast soft shadows across their faces. As the black-and-white film played, Edward leaned in and whispered, "I think I'm more interested in watching you than the movie."

Marica rolled her eyes but couldn't suppress a smile. "Then you're missing the best part."

He smirked. "I'd argue otherwise."

They cycled along the East Coast, racing each other under the shade of palm trees, her laughter carried by the sea breeze. When Edward let her win, she slowed her bike and gave him a playful glare.

"You let me win," she accused.

"I would never," he said, hand to his heart in mock offense. "You're just faster than you look."

She narrowed her eyes. "Next time, no holding back."

At the roller-skating rink, she wobbled almost immediately, gripping his hand tighter than she intended.

"I thought you said you knew how to skate," Edward teased, steadying her.

"I do," she shot back, regaining her balance. "Just... not backwards."

He laughed, effortlessly gliding beside her. "Good thing I'm here to catch you, then."

With every moment, with every shared glance and easy smile, something between them grew, something neither of them had planned, yet neither of them wanted to resist.

Chapter 9: A Moonlit Stroll by the Singapore River

The night air was thick with the scent of jasmine, sweet and intoxicating, as Marica and Edward walked side by side along the Singapore River. The city around them, illuminated by the soft glow of street lamps and the flickering lights from passing junk boats, hummed with the quiet energy of a place in constant transition. There was a calmness in the air tonight, but it wasn't the kind of stillness Marica had grown accustomed to. This felt like the calm before a storm, a storm of possibility.

They had been dating for six months, though at times it felt like much longer. Edward, with his quiet intensity, had come into her life like a rush of wind, sweeping everything up in its wake. She hadn't expected to fall for him, not this quickly, not this deeply. But with every shared moment, every laugh, every glance, he was slowly carving a space for himself in her heart.

The sound of their footsteps echoed along the river, a soft, rhythmic beat in tune with the world around them. She had been hesitant at first, after all, he was a man of the world, a stranger in a way. Yet, something about him had drawn her in from the beginning. The way he listened. The way his gaze lingered on her, as though she were the only thing that mattered. And now, here they were, together, moving through the city like they had always belonged in each other's orbit.

"Singapore is quite different from Cornwall," Edward said, his voice thoughtful as his hands tucked into his pockets, the faintest hint of a smile playing at the corner of his lips.

Marica glanced up at him, a teasing note in her voice. "In a good way or a bad way?"

He turned to her, his blue eyes glimmering in the light. "In a fascinating way," he replied, his voice low and rich, as though savouring the thought.

She tilted her head, intrigued. "What do you mean?"

Edward's gaze swept the streets around them, as though drinking in the life of the city. "It's a city in transition," he mused, his voice soft but full of conviction. "It has a kind of restless energy, like it's searching for its place in the world. Back home in Cornwall, everything feels… timeless. The cliffs, the sea, the fishing villages, they've stood the test of time, unchanged. "But here, everything feels alive, evolving, always in the process of becoming something new."

Marica's heart skipped a beat at his words. She had always seen Singapore as a place in constant change, but hearing it from him, someone who had seen the world, made it feel like something more. A city that wasn't just moving but evolving into something greater.

She met his gaze. "Not bad for an Air Force man. I didn't expect such a poetic observation."

Edward chuckled, a rich, warm sound that seemed to melt the night air around them. "We're full of surprises, you know."

Marica raised an eyebrow. "I'll believe that when I see it."

They passed a small café, the air filled with the sounds of a live band playing a soft, jazzy tune. The smooth notes of the saxophone blended with the soft murmur of voices and the clink of glasses. A few couples swayed in time to the music, their laughter carried on the breeze. The world felt impossibly far away as they continued to walk, their steps in sync, their hands brushing occasionally.

Edward stopped and turned toward her, his face soft with a mixture of tenderness and mischief. "Would you care to dance?" he asked, his voice carrying the same quiet confidence she had grown to love.

Marica blinked, taken aback. "Here? Now?"

His smile deepened, the kind of smile that made her heartbeat faster. "Why not?" He held out his hand, an invitation wrapped in warmth and something else, something unspoken but undeniable.

She hesitated, her breath catching for just a moment. "I'm not sure I—"

Before she could finish, Edward gently took her hand in his, pulling her closer with the kind of ease that made everything else fade away. "Just follow my lead," he murmured, his voice steady, coaxing.

And so, beneath the canopy of stars, they danced.

It wasn't a formal dance, not the kind of waltz or slow rhythm you'd find in grand ballrooms. No, it was something more raw, more real. It was the kind of dance you shared with someone who made you forget the world, who made you feel as though there were no rules, no boundaries, just the music and the moment. Marica stumbled at first, unsure of herself, but

Edward was there, steady and patient, guiding her effortlessly, making her laugh when she tripped over her own feet.

At first, she had felt self-conscious, how could she not? But slowly, with every laugh, every twirl, every gentle nudge, she began to let go. She wasn't thinking about the future, or the past. She was only in the present, and in this present, she had never felt more alive.

The music slowed, and Edward drew her closer, their bodies moving together with a quiet rhythm. She could feel his heartbeat against hers, the warmth of his hand on her back, his breath soft against her cheek.

The world seemed to narrow, the noise of the city fading into the background until there was nothing left but the two of them, swaying under the stars.

When the song ended, Edward didn't pull away immediately. Instead, he held her close, his arms around her, and they stood there, together, in the quiet, breathing in the same air. Their faces were so close now, their breaths mingling, that Marica could feel the warmth of his skin, could see the flicker of emotion in his eyes as they held each other's gaze.

Her heart raced, her pulse quickening, and for the first time in what felt like forever, she found herself completely lost in the moment, lost in him.

"You really do like to surprise people, don't you?" she whispered, her voice hushed, almost as if speaking louder would break the fragile spell they had woven.

Edward's gaze flickered down to her lips before meeting her eyes again, his expression unreadable. "Only when I meet someone worth surprising," he murmured, his voice low, sincere.

And in that moment, as they stood beneath the stars, Marica realized that she had fallen harder than she had ever intended to, and for the first time in a long time, she didn't want to stop.

Because, somehow, she knew that this was just the beginning.

Finally, Marica pulled back slightly, her hands still resting on his chest. "You know," she said softly, her voice tinged with a hint of playfulness, "you're making me forget I'm supposed to be keeping my distance."

Edward smiled, a hint of mischief in his eyes. "I'm not trying to make it easy for you."

Marica tilted her head, eyes narrowing slightly. "Why is that?"

Edward's smile softened. "Because I like surprises, and I like you, Marica."

The sincerity in his voice caught her off guard. She swallowed, unsure of how to respond. But before she could speak, Edward turned slightly, pulling her to the railing along the river.

"There's something I've been meaning to tell you" He began, his voice steady, though there was a touch of hesitation in his eyes.

Marica raised an eyebrow, her heart fluttering in her chest. "What's that?"

He glanced out at the river, the moonlight reflecting off the water like a silver ribbon. "You know, back in Cornwall, the sea was always there. The cliffs, the mist, it's like a different world.

I used to walk along the shore as a boy, imagining what life would be like elsewhere. I dreamed of far-off places, but never thought I'd actually leave."

Marica listened intently, sensing there was more he wanted to share.

"On stormy nights, the wind howled through the cliffs. I remember one night in particular, the thunder cracked across the sky, and the waves crashed so loudly I could barely hear myself think. But there was something comforting about it. The sea had this power, this *force* that made me feel small in comparison, yet it always made me feel safe."

Edward turned to her, his blue eyes reflecting the light of the moon. "I left Cornwall, but I think a part of me has always stayed there. Even now, when I'm far away, I sometimes hear the waves in my mind."

Marica was quiet for a moment, her gaze soft. "That sounds... beautiful. And strange, in a way."

Edward chuckled lightly, a trace of nostalgia in his voice. "Maybe. But it's home. It's who I am."

She smiled, a thought forming in her mind. "I guess you're just a bit of a romantic then."

He grinned, his eyes twinkling. "Maybe. I'm also a man who believes in second chances."

Marica looked up at him, her heart thumping in her chest. "Second chances?"

Edward nodded, his expression growing more serious. "I'm not just talking about life. I'm talking about love. Sometimes, we meet someone, and it feels like fate... like the world's been trying to bring us together all along."

Her breath caught, and she couldn't help but laugh nervously. "That sounds like a lot to put on the table."

"I've never been good at doing things halfway," Edward said, his voice low and sincere. "And I've never been good at waiting for the right moment to say what's on my mind. So here it is, I'm here in Singapore, but a part of me feels like I'm exactly where I'm supposed to be."

The air between them felt charged now, full of something unspoken, something real. Edward took a step closer, his hand brushing her cheek. "And I think you're someone I could spend the rest of my life getting to know. If you'd let me."

Marica blinked, overwhelmed by the words that hung in the air. She had never been one to believe in love at first sight, but there was something about Edward, his openness, his honesty, which made her wonder if maybe, just maybe, she was experiencing something she'd never imagined.

Her heart fluttered in her chest. "Edward..."

Before she could finish her sentence, he leaned in slowly, brushing his lips against hers in a kiss that was gentle, yet full of promise. As they pulled back, the moment felt timeless, like the sea Edward had once known, vast and all encompassing.

"I've never been good at waiting," Edward whispered, his voice brimming with hope. "So, Marica... would you make my life complete? Will you marry me?"

Marica's breath hitched, her heart pounding as if time itself had frozen. She stared at Edward, his eyes filled with love and anticipation, unaware of the beautiful coincidence unfolding before them.

Tonight wasn't just any night.

It was February 14th, her birthday.

For years, she had kept the day to herself, letting Valentine's Day overshadow it. Friends and colleagues would be swept up in their own romantic plans, leaving her to celebrate quietly, never one for grand gestures or attention. It had become her little secret.

And yet, here was Edward, on one knee, proposing on the very day she had always held close to her heart.

A breathless laugh escaped her, tears brimming in her eyes.

"Edward," she whispered, voice trembling. "Do you know what today is?"

He blinked, momentarily thrown, then glanced around at the setting, the glowing city lights, the river reflecting the soft shimmer of the night. "Valentine's Day?"

Marica nodded, biting her lip before smiling. "Yes... but it's also my birthday."

His eyes widened. "Wait, what?"

She laughed, wiping away a stray tear. "I never told you because I don't usually make a big deal out of it. But now… this," she gestured at him, at the ring, at the moment suspended between them, "this is the best birthday gift I could have ever imagined."

Edward exhaled in disbelief before a slow smile spread across his face. "So, I just accidentally planned the most meaningful proposal of your life on your birthday without even knowing it?"

She nodded, laughing through her tears.

He chuckled, shaking his head. "Well, I guess some things are just meant to be."

Marica felt her heart swell. It wasn't just the proposal it was the serendipity, the perfect timing, the universe aligning in ways she could never have predicted. This moment had been waiting for them all along.

Looking into Edward's eyes, she felt the answer bloom in her heart before she even spoke.

"Yes," she whispered, then louder, stronger, "Yes, Edward! I will marry you!"

As he slipped the ring onto her finger, the world around them blurred. It was just the two of them, standing on the edge of forever on a birthday, on a Valentine's Day, on the night that would mark the beginning of the rest of their lives.

For the first time, Marica wasn't shy about celebrating her birthday. Because now, it would always be the day she said yes to the love of her life.

Later, as they stood by the river, the moon casting silver ripples over the water, Marica found herself lost in thought. The cool night breeze rustled through the trees, but the weight in her chest felt heavier than anything the night could offer.

She had spent years guarding her heart, locking away emotions behind walls she had built for protection. Yet, nothing had prepared her for Edward the way he had slipped past her defences, the way he had made her believe in something she had long been afraid to trust.

Could she truly let go of the past?

She closed her eyes, inhaling deeply. Doubts stirred inside her. Love was unpredictable, and her scars weren't so easily erased.

Then, Edward's warm hand brushed against her cheek, pulling her back to the present. His touch was steady, grounding her. She looked up, finding patience in his gaze, a quiet understanding that both unsettled and comforted her.

"I never imagined this," she admitted. "I never thought I'd find someone who made me feel this way."

Edward's smile deepened. "I never thought I'd find someone like you either. But here we are. And maybe… this is exactly where we're meant to be."

Her breath caught, the world shrinking down to just the two of them. The river lapped softly at the shore, the night standing as a silent witness to the moment unfolding between them.

"I've spent so long keeping people out," she confessed. "I didn't know how to let anyone in. But with you, Edward... It feels different. It feels safe."

He tightened his hold on her hand, his thumb brushing gently against her skin. "You don't have to be anything other than yourself with me, Marica. I just want to be part of your life, the way you're already part of mine."

The words, simple yet profound, unravelled something deep inside her. Tears welled in her eyes, not from fear, but from the sheer weight of everything she had been holding in for so long.

"I didn't think it was possible," she whispered, "to love someone like this. But now... now I know it is. And it's terrifying, but also... freeing."

Edward stepped closer, his arms open as if to catch her, to hold her, to let her know she wasn't alone. "You don't have to be scared," he murmured. "Not with me. I promise."

And in that promise, something shifted. The walls she had kept up for so long began to crumble. The future, once shrouded in uncertainty, no longer felt so daunting.

"Is this real?" she asked, as if saying it aloud might shatter the illusion.

Edward's voice was unwavering. "It's as real as the stars above us. As real as my love for you."

Before she could respond, he kissed her. Soft at first, then deeper, as if years of unspoken words, of hidden emotions, had finally found their voice.

When they pulled away, his eyes shone with something more than joy, an unshakable certainty.

"I love you, Marica," he said, his voice thick with emotion. "I've loved you since the moment I saw you at the airport. And every day since, my feelings have only grown stronger."

Her heart clenched at the depth of his words. She had never expected this, to be loved so wholly, so completely.

"I love you too, Edward," she said, the words trembling but sure. It was as if they had been waiting to be spoken all along. "I love you."

A slow, relieved smile spread across his face.

This love wasn't just the beginning of something new. It had always been there, quietly growing, waiting for its moment to bloom.

Edward pulled her close, lifting her off her feet as laughter spilled between them, light, unburdened, joyful. The world around them faded, leaving only the two of them in a moment that felt like magic.

When he set her down, his hands remained on her waist, unwilling to let go. His fingers brushed her cheek, his voice a whisper against the cool night air.

"I've waited for this," he said. "For us. For this moment."

And then he kissed her again. Slow. Deliberate. A promise sealed between them.

As they stood there, the river murmuring beside them, the night wrapped them in quiet certainty. The future was still unknown, but for the first time, Marica wasn't afraid.

With Edward by her side, she knew they would face whatever came next, together.

Chapter 10: Wedding Preparations and Family Blessings

As the days turned into weeks, the excitement of their engagement continued to build, like a symphony reaching its crescendo. Marica and Edward poured their hearts into every detail of their wedding plans, each decision deepening their connection. From choosing the perfect date to selecting a venue that felt as if it was made for them, everything was falling into place as if the universe was aligning in their favour.

Edward, who had always been drawn to Singapore's rich cultural and architectural heritage, knew he wanted their wedding to reflect both their love story and the city they now called home. After much discussion, they decided on Saint Andrew's Cathedral, a majestic symbol of Singapore's history and a place where love, faith, and timeless beauty converged. Built in 1861, the cathedral's iconic white façade, its towering spires reaching toward the sky like a prayer, seemed like the perfect place to begin their new life together.

But there was one moment Marica had been anxiously awaiting: the blessing of her mother. Marica had always been close to her mother, a woman whose unwavering support had seen her through every chapter of her life. Her mother had been her guiding star, the one constant who stood by her during moments of doubt, and the person she turned to for comfort in times of joy and sorrow. From the first time Marica had scraped her knee to the day she moved away to begin her own life, her mother's love had been a steady force.

She had always dreamed of hearing her mother's blessing before stepping into this next phase of her journey. This was a turning point in her life, and Marica needed her mother's approval more than anything, even though deep down, she knew her love for Edward was enough to carry her forward.

That Sunday afternoon, with the weight of the moment heavy in her chest, Marica invited her mother over to share the news.

Sitting together on the couch, Marica's mother cradled a cup of tea in her hands, her gaze warm and open as she listened to her daughter's words. The sunlight filtered through the windows, casting a soft glow on the room as Marica took a deep breath, her heart pounding in her chest. She had always valued her mother's opinions, but now, with the prospect of marriage on the horizon, she couldn't help but wonder what her mother would think. She felt the weight of the decision, this was not just about a wedding, but a union of two lives, two families, and a future that was still unfolding.

"Mother," she began, her voice trembling slightly but steady, "there's something I need to share with you. Edward proposed to me, and I said yes."

Her mother's eyes widened in surprise, but a smile spread across her face, soft and tender. The joy in her eyes mirrored the emotion building inside Marica. Without saying a word, her mother rose and embraced her, enveloping her in a cocoon of love and warmth. For a moment, Marica closed her eyes and allowed herself to savour the feeling, this moment, this connection, this shared bond that had withstood the tests of time.

"Oh, Marica," her mother whispered. "I'm so happy for you. I've seen the way Edward looks at you, and I can see he loves you with all his heart. You deserve every bit of happiness."

Marica's heart swelled, her eyes brimming with tears as she clung to her mother, feeling a mix of relief and joy. She had feared that her mother might have doubts, might have held onto her own expectations for Marica's life. But now, in this quiet embrace, she knew that her mother's approval was everything.

It was more than just the wedding. This was the culmination of a lifetime of love, guidance, and sacrifice. Her mother had been there for her in all the small, tender moments, the sleepless nights as a child, the quiet encouragement as an adult and now, she was giving her blessing to this new chapter. Marica realised that this was not just a new beginning for her and Edward, but also a new phase in her relationship with her mother.

"I wouldn't miss your wedding for the world," her mother continued, pulling away just slightly, her hands resting on Marica's shoulders. "I'll be right by your side, darling."

As Marica looked into her mother's eyes, she could see the depth of her love, the quiet pride, and the hope she had always had for Marica's happiness.

It was as if the baton had been passed, and Marica now had the chance to create her own future, just as her mother had done for her.

Marica thought back to all the years when she had felt uncertain about her place in the world, but her mother's steady presence had always been a reminder that love and trust were the foundation of everything. And now, as she prepared to marry Edward, she felt that same sense of unwavering support, not only from her mother, but from herself as well.

"I'm so grateful for you," Marica whispered, her voice full of emotion. "Thank you for always being there for me. I wouldn't be who I am without you."

Her mother smiled, her eyes softening with tenderness. "And I'm so proud of the woman you've become. You've always had a strong heart, Marica. You know how to love, and that's all that matters."

In that moment, Marica felt a deep peace settle within her. She was stepping into a new chapter, but her roots, her foundation, were firmly grounded in the love and wisdom her mother had passed down. And with that, she felt ready to begin this journey with Edward by her side.

The future was still unknown, but one thing was certain, she had her mother's blessing, and with it, the courage to embrace whatever came next.

Chapter 11: The Wedding Day

The morning of the wedding arrived like a dream, the sky an unblemished blue, the sun gentle and warm, casting a golden light over the world below. The breeze whispered through the leaves of the cathedral garden, the fragrance of blooming flowers adding to the beauty of the day. Marica stood in the back of the church, the soft rustle of her dress the only sound as she prepared to walk down the aisle. Her heart fluttered with a combination of excitement and nervousness, her fingers trembling slightly as she smoothed the delicate lace of her wedding gown.

Saint Andrew's Cathedral stood before her like something out of a storybook. Its towering white columns seemed to stretch toward the heavens, its steeples piercing the sky in graceful spires. Inside, the air was filled with the rich scent of polished wood and the faint smell of incense, the glow from the stained-glass windows casting colourful light onto the pews. The cathedral, a perfect blend of history and elegance, was more than just a place; it was a sanctuary, a testament to the sacredness of their love and the promise of their future together.

Edward stood at the altar, waiting for her. His eyes were locked on the doors, his hands clasped together in silent prayer. The anticipation was almost unbearable, but when the doors opened, the moment seemed to stop.

Marica stood on the threshold, bathed in the soft light of the cathedral, her presence ethereal. She wore a gown that was both timeless and modern, an elegant creation of silk and lace that hugged her frame, the soft ivory fabric catching the light with every step. The bodice was adorned with delicate lace, which cascaded into a flowing skirt that moved like liquid around her feet. A veil, light as air, framed her face, her hair styled in soft waves that shimmered as she moved. She was a vision, radiant, and Edward's breath caught in his throat.

Her mother walked beside her, her grip firm yet tender, a quiet strength guiding her forward. It should have been her father. She had dreamed of this moment as a little girl, imagined the steady warmth of his hand in hers, the quiet pride in his eyes as he gave her away. But life had rewritten that story long ago. The war had taken him before she could form real memories of him, before he could see the woman she had become.

And yet, in the hush of the chapel, she felt him. In the way the light streamed through the stained-glass windows, warm and golden, in the whisper of the breeze through the open doors, as if carrying his voice from some distant place. He was here. He had always been here.

When they reached the altar, her mother turned to her, eyes filled with love, before gently placing her hand in his. He took it without hesitation, his fingers warm, grounding her, anchoring her to this moment. His eyes searched hers, filled with something deep and knowing.

"He'd be proud of you," he murmured, his voice rough with emotion, as if he could see the thoughts swirling in her heart.

A lump rose in her throat, but she smiled, blinking away the tears. She had always known it. In the quiet spaces of her soul, she had felt his pride, his love, wrapped around her like an unbreakable thread.

"I know," she whispered.

And as she stood there, her hand in his, love wrapped around her in every form, she realized something, this moment, this love, was everything her father had ever wanted for her.

As Marica spoke, her voice was steady despite the tears glistening in her eyes, each word carrying the weight of the love they had built, the life they were about to begin. The chapel was silent, as if the world itself was holding its breath, witnessing something rare, something unshakable.

Edward's fingers tightened around hers, his touch warm, reassuring, as if he were memorizing the feel of this moment, locking it away deep in his heart. The golden light from the stained-glass windows bathed them both, casting soft hues of red and gold over their joined hands, over the promises they had just made.

Marica turned briefly, catching her mother's gaze. There were tears in her mother's eyes, a mix of joy and the bittersweet ache of a love remembered. Her father wasn't here to give her away, but in every step she had taken down that aisle, she had felt him. She knew, without a doubt, that if he were standing in this room, he would be proud.

Edward's voice, thick with emotion, pulled her back to the moment. His eyes never left hers as he spoke, each word a vow, a promise carved into forever.

"You are my heart, Marica," he said, his voice trembling slightly, as if the depth of his love couldn't be contained. "Today, and every day after, I promise to love you. Through every moment, through every joy and every challenge, I will be by your side. I will hold you, protect you, and cherish you. You are my everything."

Marica's breath caught, her heart swelling with love and gratitude. She squeezed his hands, her voice thick with emotion as she looked into his eyes.

"And I promise to love you, always," she whispered. "With every part of me, I will stand by you. I promise to support you, to grow with you, and to never let go of the love we share. I will walk beside you, through the brightest days and the darkest nights, knowing that if we are together, we have everything we need. Today marks the beginning of our forever."

A single tear slipped down her cheek, but Edward was already there, brushing it away with the pad of his thumb.

"You are my forever," he murmured.

In that instant, time felt suspended, the past and the future converging into this one perfect second.

Marica thought of everything that had brought them here, the laughter, the quiet moments, the challenges that had only made them stronger. And somewhere, in the quiet corners of her heart, she felt her father's presence, steady and proud.

"You are my heart, too," she whispered, her voice barely audible but meant only for him.

The vows lingered in the air, sacred and unbreakable, binding their hearts together in a promise that would last a lifetime. The rest of the ceremony passed in a beautiful blur, the soft hum of whispered blessings, the warmth of their joined hands, the quiet tremor of love in every glance. And then, at last, the moment came.

When they were pronounced husband and wife, Edward pulled her close, his lips brushing against hers in a kiss that was tender at first, then deepened with the full weight of his love. The cathedral erupted into applause, the joyful sound echoing through the grand stone walls, wrapping around them like an embrace.

As they stepped outside, hand in hand, the golden afternoon sunbathed them in warmth. A canopy had been set up just beyond the church doors, its flowing white fabric billowing softly in the breeze. Beneath it, long tables adorned with fresh roses and flickering candles stretched out, surrounded by family and friends who cheered as the newlyweds emerged.

Marica's mother stood near the entrance, her eyes shining with pride and love.

When she embraced her daughter, it was as if the warmth of her father's presence was there, wrapping around them both, whispering of his pride and love from beyond.

The celebration unfolded beneath the open sky, the scent of lavender and fresh-cut flowers carried on the breeze. Glasses clinked in joyful toasts, laughter rippled through the gathering, and music played softly, weaving through the evening air like a melody of love.

As the sun dipped lower, painting the sky in hues of amber and violet, Marica and Edward took to the dance floor beneath the twinkling lights strung through the canopy. Wrapped in his arms, she let herself melt into the moment, the warmth of his touch, the way he looked at her like she was the only thing that mattered.

"Are you happy?" he murmured, his voice just for her.

She smiled, her heart swelling. "More than I ever imagined."

As the night wore on, stories were shared, old memories relived, and new ones created. Their love was celebrated in every embrace, every laugh, every whispered promise. And as Edward pulled her close beneath the soft glow of lanterns, he pressed a kiss to her temple, his voice steady and full of certainty.

"This is just the beginning, Marica. Our forever starts now."

And as she leaned into him, she knew, no matter what lay ahead, they would face it together. Always.

Chapter 12: A Night on Sentosa

The night air was warm, filled with the calming scent of the ocean, and the sound of gentle waves lapping against the shore seemed to echo the rhythm of their hearts. After the whirlwind of their wedding day, the vows, the laughter, the promises, Marica and Edward found themselves in the soft embrace of the evening, alone at last, on the island of Sentosa.

Their wedding had been everything they had hoped for, but now, with the world quieting down around them, they were ready to begin their new life together. The island at night was breathtaking, the lights sparkling like stars in the distance, and the water crashing softly against the rocks beneath their private villa, filling the air with a tranquil melody.

The villa was an idyllic retreat perched right on the edge of the beach. The large windows framed an endless view of the sea, and as Marica stepped through the door, she inhaled deeply, letting the salty air fill her lungs. The room was bathed in the soft glow of candles, their flickering flames dancing on the walls, casting shadows that seemed to create a world of their own, a world where only the two of them existed.

Edward stood by the window, his back to her, gazing out at the vast expanse of water. The moonlight poured across the waves like silver ribbons, the night serene except for the distant tide rolling in. His wedding suit had been discarded, leaving him in just his trousers, his shirt untucked, the top few buttons undone. His sleeves were rolled up, exposing the strong lines of his forearms, silent testament to the man he had become, the man who was now hers.

Marica stood in the doorway, her heart swelling. Gone was her wedding gown, the lace and silk gently draped across a nearby chair. Now, she wore something softer, more intimate, a flowing ivory nightgown, the delicate straps resting gracefully on her shoulders, the fabric whispering against her skin. The moonlight illuminated the gown's soft folds, casting a glow over her, making her look almost ethereal. Her hair, once pinned in an elegant updo, now tumbled in loose waves down her back, strands framing her face.

Edward turned as if he sensed her presence. For a moment, his breath caught in his chest when he saw her standing in the doorway, illuminated by the moonlight, radiating beauty in a way that took his breath away.

"You're beautiful," he murmured, his voice husky, thick with emotion.

A soft smile touched her lips, her gaze softening as she stepped toward him. Barefoot against the wooden floor, the silk of her gown trailing behind her, she reached up to touch his face, her fingers tracing the strong line of his jaw. "And you're my husband now," she whispered, the words filled with wonder.

Edward's hand found her waist, pulling her close, his thumb brushing over the smooth satin of her nightgown. "Forever," he promised, sealing the vow with a kiss, a kiss that was slow, deep, and filled with the weight of everything they had been through to reach this moment. It wasn't just a kiss, it was a promise, a seal on the life they were about to build together.

When they finally pulled away, breathless, Marica's fingers traced the strong lines of his jaw, her eyes filled with wonder. "I still can't believe this is real," she murmured, her voice thick with emotion.

Edward smiled gently, tucking a stray lock of hair behind her ear. "It's more real than anything I've ever known," he whispered, his voice steady, as though grounding them both in this new reality.

She gazed up at him, her heart full, but there was something more in her eyes, something unspoken. A quiet vulnerability lingered there, a hesitation, a touch of uncertainty born of the unknown.

Sensing it, Edward cupped her cheek with a tenderness that made her chest ache. "Marica," he murmured, his voice soft, "you don't have to be nervous."

She swallowed, a blush rising on her cheeks as she nodded, her voice barely above a whisper. "It's just… I've never done this before," she confessed, her gaze lowered in a mixture of shyness and trust.

A flicker of understanding passed through Edward's eyes, and he ran his fingers gently down her arm. "Then we'll take our time," he promised, his voice low and reassuring. "Tonight isn't about anything except us, just you and me."

Marica let out a shaky breath, feeling the weight of his words settle in her heart. She trusted him completely, in every way. "I trust you, Edward. I always have."

The world outside seemed to disappear, leaving only the two of them, bound by something deeper than words. Edward gently took her hand and led her to the bed, the soft sheets welcoming them. They lay together, and Marica felt the tenderness in every touch, every moment of his patience. She felt the way he cherished her, guiding her through the intimacy of the night, making every second feel sacred. As their bodies came together for the first time, it was more than an act, it was a bond, a promise sealed with love.

Afterward, they lay in each other's arms, the cool night air brushing against their skin. The only sounds were their quiet breathing and the rhythmic lull of the ocean outside.

Edward brushed his fingers through Marica's hair, his voice soft and filled with awe. "I never thought I could love you more than I already did... but tonight, you've shown me just how deep love can go."

She smiled, her hand resting over his heart, feeling its steady beat beneath her palm. "And I'll keep showing you, Edward. Every day, for the rest of our lives."

Outside, the stars glittered above the vast sea, their endless light reflected in the peaceful stillness of the night. Their vows had been spoken in the church, but now, in the quiet intimacy of their wedding night, they made them again, wordlessly, through touch, through love, through the certainty that they belonged to each other.

The night stretched ahead of them, filled with whispered promises, a love unbreakable by time or circumstance. And as Edward held her close, pressing a final, tender kiss to her forehead, they both knew, this was just the beginning.

Chapter 13: The Move to Cornwall

After the honeymoon, life takes a surprising turn for Marica. What was supposed to be the start of a beautiful new chapter soon becomes a tangled web of conflicting emotions. Edward's work posting brings them to Cornwall, a place as foreign to Marica as a far-off dream. She had imagined adventures and excitement, but what awaited her was a peaceful, quiet life in the heart of the British countryside.

The bustling energy of Singapore, where she had spent most of her life, feels like a lifetime ago now. She had always been surrounded by vibrant street markets, the hum of busy cafes, the bright lights of the city, and her beloved mother, who had been her anchor in the storm of life. And now? She's standing at the edge of a rolling green landscape, the fields stretching for miles, with only the occasional sheep to break the silence.

It's a jarring contrast.

The first few weeks are the hardest for Marica. As Edward excitedly immerses himself in his work and the charm of Cornwall, she finds herself in a world of solitude. The locals, though warm and friendly, seem to exist in a rhythm she hasn't quite figured out. Their words are softer, their pace slower, and their traditions are all so new to her.

Marica feels like she's an outsider, a woman disconnected from her roots, adrift in a place where she doesn't belong.

One evening, as the mist settles over the hills and the quiet of Cornwall presses in, Marica finds herself by the window of their small cottage, her hands cradling a warm mug of tea. The rain taps gently on the glass, a comforting sound, yet it only deepens the weight in her chest.

"I miss Singapore," Marica murmurs, to herself, as her gaze sweeps over the misty hills. "It's just… so quiet here, Edward. So... lonely. I feel like everything is slipping away, like I've left part of myself behind."

Edward, who's adjusting to this slower life with ease, stands behind her, leaning against the doorframe. He watches her, a mix of concern and love in his eyes. "I know, love. I can see it. You're struggling. But you'll find your place here, I promise. It's going to take time. We've been through a lot already, and we'll get through this too."

Marica shakes her head, her voice thick with emotion. "But it's not just the quiet, Edward. It's… my mother. I feel like I've abandoned her. I left everything, my friends, my life, my mother, and now I'm here, in this strange, new place. It's not just homesickness, it's this... emptiness."

Edward steps closer, his voice gentle, his arms wrapping around her. "You didn't abandon anyone. Your mom knows how much you love her. She'll understand that this is part of our journey, just like I do. This is where our future is, together. And we'll find a way to make it home for both of us, even if it's different than what you're used to."

Marica leans into him, taking comfort in his warmth, but her thoughts still drift back to her mother, to the life she left behind in Singapore. She had always been so close to her, sharing everything, her worries, her dreams, her heart. And now, the distance feels insurmountable.

"I just… I don't know how to let go, Edward. How do I start fresh here when my heart is still in Singapore? I talk to Mum every day, but it's not the same. She's not here to help me through this." Her voice breaks, and she wipes away a tear that slips down her cheek.

Edward holds her tighter, pressing his lips gently to her hair. "I know, darling. I know. It's not easy, I understand that. But you're not alone in this. You've got me. You've got us. And we'll build something here, something new, something beautiful. It won't replace everything, but it will be ours. I know that's not much right now, but I believe in us. I believe in you."

She looks up at him, her eyes searching for any hint of doubt, but all she finds is unwavering love. It gives her the courage to breathe, to release the tension that has been building in her chest.

"I want to believe in it too," she says softly. "I really do. But it feels like there's so much to let go of. I don't know where to begin."

Edward cups her face gently, brushing away a few stray tears. "It's okay to take it slow, Marica. We'll take it one step at a time. You're not alone in this. And as for your mum... she's a part of you, and no matter where you are, that will never change."

Marica nods, leaning into him for a moment longer, then pulling away slightly. "I think… I think I just need to make this place feel like home. To find a piece of myself here. With you."

Edward smiles, a tender look in his eyes. "We'll do it together. And soon, you'll see, Cornwall will feel like home too. Not in the way Singapore was, but in its own distinct way. And in the meantime, we have all the time in the world to make this place ours."

The quiet of Cornwall surrounds them, but it no longer feels so lonely. In his arms, Marica begins to feel a small flicker of hope. Maybe, just maybe, she could learn to love this place, to make it her own. After all, her heart was with Edward, and with him by her side, she knew they would find their way.

As the evening stretched on, the fire in the hearth crackled softly, casting a warm glow across the room. The rain had stopped, but the cool air lingered outside, adding to the comfort of their cottage. Marica leaned against Edward, her heart full of the love she had for him, and the depth of the bond they shared.

In that quiet moment, with the flickering light from the fire illuminating their faces, Marica's hand found its way to Edward's chest, feeling the steady rhythm of his heartbeat. There was an undeniable connection between them, something so deep, so powerful, it seemed to transcend words. The uncertainty of the past few weeks melted away, and in its place, there was only the warmth of their love.

Edward's gaze softened, and he gently lifted her chin to meet his eyes. Without a word, he leaned down, capturing her lips in a kiss that spoke of longing, of reassurance, and of the promise of a future they would build together. The kiss deepened, a silent agreement passing between them, a reminder that they weren't just partners in life, but lovers in every sense.

They moved together toward the fireplace, the flames dancing in their eyes, casting shadows on the walls. In the intimacy of their cottage, surrounded by the soft hum of the night and the warmth of the fire, they made love with a passion so raw, so deep, it was as if they were binding themselves to each other once more, affirming the strength of their connection.

Marica closed her eyes, lost in the feeling of Edward's touch, of the love that filled the space between them. It was a love that had already weathered storms, a love that would continue to grow as they faced life's challenges together. And in that moment, as they held each other close by the firelight, Marica knew that no matter where life took them, their love would always be their anchor.

Chapter 14: A Cottage by the Sea

Saint Ives had always been one of those places where time seemed to slow down, where the world felt a little softer, a little warmer. Marica and Edward had never intended to settle there, but sometimes life had a way of surprising you, nudging you toward the things you didn't know you were meant to find.

One afternoon, while they wandered through the village hand-in-hand, they stumbled upon a small cottage that seemed to call to them in a way neither of them could explain. It was tucked away just far enough from the village centre, overlooking the endless stretch of the sea, the waves crashing softly against the cliffs in the distance. The cottage, with its weathered stone walls and ivy that clung to the façade like the embrace of an old friend, felt as though it had been waiting for them.

The windows were slightly askew, their panes old and scratched from years of catching the salty sea air. The floors creaked with each step they took, almost as if the house was sharing its stories, quiet, beautiful stories from days gone by. Inside, the rooms were small but filled with warmth and charm. There were two bedrooms, a tiny kitchen where Marica could already imagine herself cooking, and a living room with a fireplace that seemed to whisper promises of cozy nights, curled up together by the fire.

It was simple, but it was perfect.

The garden out back was modest, with a patch of soil that seemed eager to grow whatever they planted. It was the kind of place where they could picture themselves together, Edward in the mornings, planting vegetables, while Marica, with her green thumb, tended to the herbs and flowers. A life built from the earth and sea, one that felt as though it had always been meant to be theirs.

The cottage wasn't just a house, it was a memory, a promise, a future waiting to be written. And when the old man who owned the house told them its story, they understood why.

His wife had passed away not long ago, and the house had become too quiet, too empty for him to stay. But when he met Edward and Marica, something in the way they spoke about the house, about how they looked at each other, reminded him of the love he had shared with his wife. He saw in them the same spark, the same tenderness, the same joy he and his wife once shared. And so, without hesitation, he offered them the house at a price far below what it was worth.

"You two… your love," he said, his voice thick with emotion, "it reminds me of what I had with my wife. I want this house to have life in it again. I want it to be filled with love. Please… take care of it."

They didn't need to say a word. The look that passed between them said everything.

In that moment, everything felt right. The world outside faded, and all they could hear was the sound of their hearts beating in unison.

Later, they stood outside the cottage, the wind coming off the sea, the scent of salt in the air, and the sun beginning to set in a wash of orange and pink across the sky. They could hear the sound of the waves crashing against the shore, the same sound that would lull them to sleep every night in their new home. The garden stretched out before them, the promise of fresh fruit, herbs, and vegetables growing beneath their fingertips.

For the first time in a long while, they felt the weight of a shared future, the kind of future they'd dreamed of, together.

And as they stood there, side by side, Edward took her hand in his and whispered, "We're going to make this place ours. Together."

Marica smiled, feeling the truth of his words in her bones. They had found their place. And in it, they would build everything they had ever wanted, a life of love, of peace, of home.

They dove into their new life, day by day, each moment pulling them deeper into a shared dream. The work on the cottage wasn't just about fixing walls or hammering nails; it was about creating something that felt like their own. Each brushstroke, each swing of the hammer, was like breathing life back into the space, transforming it into more than just a house, it was becoming their story. There was magic in restoring something worn and weathered, giving it new meaning. The old wood beneath their feet creaked, a subtle reminder of the past, while each new coat of paint seemed to brighten not only the walls but the future they were building together.

As the days passed, the garden bloomed too, like a testament to their hard work. What had once been a wild mess of weeds and brambles was now a place of quiet beauty. Marica carefully planted roses, their delicate petals unfurling in the warm breeze, as if echoing the new life they were growing together. Lavender swayed gently, a fragrant reminder of the peace they were finding. The air was thick with the smell of earth, fresh growth, and possibility.

But it wasn't just the work that made the cottage feel like home, it was the quiet moments, too. The evenings when they'd step back, look at what they'd accomplished, and just hold each other.

The golden hour, when the sun dipped low and bathed everything in a soft, amber glow, became their time to savour. Without a word, they'd fall into each other's arms, letting the world outside fall away. In those moments, the love they shared felt as real and tangible as the walls they were rebuilding.

One evening, as they worked on the living room wall, Edward struggled to hang a picture frame. His brow furrowed in frustration, his voice tinged with exasperation.

"Why do all these old cottages have to be so crooked?" he muttered, trying again to align the frame exactly right.

Marica leaned against the doorframe, a teasing smile playing on her lips. "It's not crooked, it's charming," she said, her eyes dancing with mischief. "I think it gives the place character."

Edward shot her a playful look, his frustration slipping away. "Character?" he laughed. "This place is leaning more than I am after a few too many pints on a Friday night."

She laughed with him, stepping closer to adjust the frame herself. But as soon as her fingers touched it, it swung out of alignment again.

"Well, maybe that's because you're holding it crooked," she teased, her fingers brushing against his as they both tried to fix it.

Edward sighed dramatically, shaking his head. "I didn't think my quiet life in Cornwall would come with a full-on renovation project."

Marica chuckled, the sound light and carefree. "Oh, but you did. You just didn't know it yet. Welcome to my world, love."

Edward grinned, pulling her closer, his arm wrapping around her waist. "And I wouldn't have it any other way." He kissed her forehead, the simple act carrying so much meaning. "It's worth it, though, isn't it? All of this? Building our life here?"

Marica nodded, her heart full as she looked at him. "More than worth it. This place isn't perfect, but it's ours. And that's all that matters."

They stood there together, in the heart of their little cottage. The air was thick with the scent of fresh paint and wood, the crackling fire casting a warm glow over the space they were turning into their home.

"Just like us," Marica murmured, her gaze soft as it met Edward's.

He raised an eyebrow, a knowing smile tugging at the corner of his lips. "What do you mean?"

She nodded toward the crooked picture frame. "This house might not be straight. It might have its flaws. But so do we. And that's what makes it beautiful."

Edward's smile softened, his heart swelling with affection for the woman standing beside him. "And we'll make it work, just like we always do, won't we?"

"Of course," she whispered, tracing the line of his jaw with her fingers. "Together, always."

In that moment, surrounded by the imperfections of their new home, their hearts beat as one. They had found something that was truly theirs, a love that would fill every corner of this crooked, wonderful place. It wasn't just a house they were building. It was a life.

And when he kissed her, soft and slow, their love became more than just a promise, it was the foundation they'd laid together. The crooked walls, the uneven floors, the beauty in every flaw, they would make it work. They always had, and they always would.

Chapter 15: A Taste of Home

Marica had walked these streets countless times before. The cobbled paths of St. Ives were familiar to her now, their twists and turns a quiet comfort in a life still adjusting to change. Yet today, something was different.

Perhaps it was the way the light hit the rooftops, casting long golden shadows across the stone. Or maybe it was the faint scent of salt in the breeze, carrying whispers of places far beyond the shores of Cornwall. Or perhaps, just perhaps, it was fate.

Because today, Marica took a turn she hadn't taken before.

And that was when she saw it.

A little shop, tucked away on a quiet street, almost as if it had been waiting for her all along. The building was unassuming, worn wooden beams, a soft blue-painted door, a faded sign whose letters had blurred with time. But through the large glass window, sunlight poured in, illuminating a forgotten space. A wooden counter stood at the back, its edges smoothed by years of hands resting there. A few tables remained, empty yet filled with possibility.

She pressed her fingers lightly against the cool glass, her reflection staring back at her. And then, something stirred within her, a whisper, a memory, a longing.

This could be something.

She closed her eyes, and at that moment, she wasn't standing in a quiet street in Cornwall anymore. She was back in Singapore, in her mother's kitchen, the scent of coconut and lemongrass thick in the air. She could hear the sizzle of oil, the rhythmic chopping of garlic, the bubbling of rich, fragrant curries.

Nasi lemak, laksa, chicken rice, and devil's curry were once the everyday meals of her childhood, but now they felt like fragments of a home she ached for.

When Marica opened her eyes, the little shop was still there, waiting. And suddenly, she knew.

This wasn't just an idea. This was her purpose.

That evening, she prepared dinner as if the act itself would prove something to her. She didn't just cook; she poured herself into the food, letting her hands move instinctively, guided by years of memories and lessons passed down through generations. The rich, heady scent of spices filled their home, wrapping around her like a warm embrace.

When Edward walked into the dining room, he stopped in his tracks. The warm glow of candlelight flickered across the room, casting soft shadows on the walls. A bottle of red wine sat in the center of the table, its deep crimson hue catching the light. The rich aroma of coconut milk and lemongrass filled the air, mingling with the savoury scent of roasted spices. Before him was a feast, one that spoke of home, love, and something more.

"Marica," he murmured, his voice laced with awe. "What's all this?"

95

She looked up, suddenly nervous. "Sit," she said softly.

He did. And then he took his first bite.

The moment his fork touched his lips, something shifted in his expression. He chewed slowly, savouring, his brows lifting in surprise. "This," he said, swallowing, "is incredible."

A soft laugh escaped her lips, but she didn't speak.

Edward set his fork down, glancing at the array of dishes before him, steaming bowls of laksa, golden-fried chicken atop fragrant rice, a pot of devil's curry, its deep red colour promising heat and depth.

"Why haven't you made all of this before?" he asked, looking at her.

She hesitated, then sighed. "I don't know," she admitted. "Maybe I didn't realise how much I needed it."

Edward studied her, his blue eyes searching hers. "Tell me", he said.

So, she did.

She told him about the shop. About the way it had made her heart race. About the idea that had taken root the moment she saw it. About the feeling, deep, unshakable, that this was what she was meant to do.

When she finished, she exhaled, suddenly aware of the silence stretching between them.

Edward didn't speak right away. He simply watched her, his gaze filled with something unreadable.

Then, slowly, he reached across the table, taking her hand in his.

"This is important to you," he said, not as a question, but as a quiet understanding.

She nodded, unable to speak past the lump in her throat.

A smile curved his lips. "Then let's do it."

Marica's breath caught. "You mean?"

"I mean, you belong here, Marica. But that doesn't mean you have to leave everything else behind. If this"—he gestured to the food, to the love she had poured into every dish—"is part of who you are, then Cornwall should know it too."

Tears stung the back of her eyes, but she blinked them away. Instead, she tightened her grip on his hand, her heart swelling with something she hadn't felt in a long time.

Hope.

Edward grinned and picked up his spoon. "Now, before we talk business, pass me more of that devil's curry, will you? It's absolutely divine."

Marica laughed, and for the first time in weeks, she felt at home.

Maybe Cornwall wasn't just where life had brought her.

Maybe it was where she was meant to build something new.

And with that thought, the next chapter of her life had begun.

Chapter 16: A Dream Takes Flight

The next six months were a whirlwind. From the moment Marica and Edward decided to turn her vision into reality, their lives became a blur of planning, late-night discussions, and endless to-do lists.

The little shop on the quiet street in St. Ives slowly transformed. Gone were the dusty shelves and worn-out counters; in their place stood a warm, inviting space that blended Singaporean charm with Cornish coziness. Marica had designed it herself, bright wooden tables, delicate Peranakan tiles lining the walls, and warm lanterns that cast a soft glow over the room. At the front, a glass display case showcased golden curry puffs, fresh pandan cakes, and crispy prawn crackers, enticing passersby.

She decided to name it *"Little Singapore"* a tribute to home, a piece of herself in this foreign land.

The grand opening was scheduled for a Saturday morning, and Marica could barely sleep the night before. She had spent weeks perfecting the menu, testing recipes in their tiny kitchen, and making sure every dish captured the authentic flavours of her childhood. She had no idea if people would come. Would the Cornish locals even be interested in Singaporean food?

She needn't have worried.

The Grand Opening

By 10 a.m., the queue had already started forming outside. Word had spread, curiosity had built up, and the scent of sizzling satay and fragrant chicken rice wafting through the streets had drawn people in like a magnet.

Marica and Edward stood side by side as he unlocked the doors for the very first time.

"Here we go," he murmured, squeezing her hand.

The moment they stepped inside, the place was filled with life. The first customers, locals who had known the shop when it was a café years ago, walked in, drawn to the unfamiliar yet irresistible aromas. Marica worked tirelessly behind the counter, serving steaming bowls of laksa, fragrant nasi lemak with crispy ikan bilis, and plates of tender Hainanese chicken rice drizzled with garlic-chili sauce.

"Try this, love," an elderly woman nudged her husband, handing him a spoonful of beef rendang. "Good heavens, this is delicious!"

A young father, holding his little boy in one arm, smiled as he took a bite of the devil's curry. The rich, spicy heat of the dish hit him first, followed by the deep, earthy flavour of the tender chicken simmered in a fragrant blend of spices and coconut milk. The heat was balanced perfectly with a hint of sweetness, the complex layers of flavour making each bite even more satisfying than the last. "Reminds me of my time in Singapore years ago," he said, his eyes lighting up with nostalgia. "You've brought something special here."

Customers kept coming, and before she knew it, Marica had completely sold out of curry puffs and kueh lapis. The kitchen was a flurry of movement, Edward managing the front, refilling drinks and chatting with customers, while Marica cooked with a fire she hadn't felt in years. The joy of sharing her food, of seeing people's delighted reactions, made every aching muscle and every sleepless night worth it.

By the end of the day, Edward counted the till and turned to her with a stunned expression.

"Marica… we've sold out of everything."

She wiped her hands on her apron, exhausted but exhilarated. "Everything?"

"Everything. Every last plate, every last bowl."

She slumped into a chair, barely believing it. "We did it."

Edward leaned down and kissed her forehead. "No, love. *You* did it."

As weeks turned into months, Little Singapore became one of the most talked-about spots in town. The once-quiet street now bustled with energy as locals and visitors alike came to experience the magic of Marica's food. Some were drawn by curiosity, others by word of mouth. Soon, even local food critics were writing about the little shop that had brought a taste of Southeast Asia to Cornwall.

Marica still insisted on cooking everything herself in the beginning. She arrived at dawn, prepping fresh ingredients, making spice pastes from scratch, and ensuring every dish tasted exactly as it should.

But as the demand grew, it became clear that she couldn't do it alone.

One evening, as she and Edward sat at their dining table going through the week's sales, he reached for her hand.

"Marica, you need help," he said gently.

She sighed. "I know, but... this is my food, my recipes. I want it to be perfect."

"And it will be. But you can't keep doing this by yourself. It's time to find people who can help you, people you can train."

Reluctantly, she agreed.

The first person she hired was an eager young woman named Sarah, who had worked in bakeries before but had never cooked Asian food. Marica trained her patiently, teaching her how to stir-fry sambal with just the right amount of heat, how to steam chicken for the perfect Hainanese chicken rice, and how to make flaky, buttery curry puffs.

Then came Raj, a university student from Malaysia who had grown up eating similar dishes and picked up her techniques quickly.

Slowly, Marica built a small but dedicated team, each of them learning and respecting the flavours she had brought to Cornwall.

The kitchen became more than just a place to cook; it became a space of laughter, of learning, of stories shared over simmering pots of broth and trays of freshly made dumplings.

And Marica, once a homesick woman in a foreign land, found herself exactly where she was meant to be.

One evening, as she wiped down the counters after a particularly busy day, she looked out through the large glass windows and saw something that made her heart swell.

A group of locals, older women, young couples, even children sitting outside on the benches, enjoying plates of char kway teow and bowls of laksa as if they had been eating them their whole lives.

She turned to Edward, who was watching her with quiet pride.

"Look at them," she whispered.

He smiled. "You brought something special to this place, Marica. You brought a piece of yourself."

Tears pricked her eyes as she leaned into his embrace.

Six months ago, she had been lost. Now, she had a thriving business, a team who felt like family, and a town that had embraced her food as their own.

And for the first time since leaving Singapore, she felt truly at home.

Chapter 17: A Growing Family

One chilly morning, after a busy shift at the restaurant, Marica stood in the kitchen, wiping her hands on her apron, the smell of chicken curry still lingering in the air. She'd been on her feet for hours, stirring pots, greeting customers, and making sure everything ran smoothly. But now, a sudden wave of dizziness swept over her. The room spun, and she grabbed the edge of the counter to steady herself. Her stomach churned, and before she knew it, she had to sit down, feeling faint.

Edward, who had been helping in the back, rushed over as he saw her pale face. "Marica?" he asked, his voice thick with concern. "Are you okay?"

"I—I'm fine," she whispered, though the tremor in her voice betrayed her. But her body wasn't so sure. She felt her stomach rebel, the familiar sensation of nausea creeping up her throat. It wasn't long before she stumbled to the restroom, barely making it in time.

Edward stood in the doorway, his expression dark with worry. He hadn't seen her like this before. She was always so full of life, so strong. Seeing her so fragile, so vulnerable, it unsettled him.

When she emerged, pale and weak, he didn't hesitate. "Let's get you home, love. You need to rest."

On the ride back, the quiet between them felt heavier than usual. Edward couldn't shake the feeling that something was wrong. Marica was never one to complain, never one to let anything hold her back. But today... Today, something felt different.

He glanced over at her, her face turned toward the window, lost in thought. He wondered what it could possibly be. Was she just exhausted from the long hours? Or was it something more? Something he didn't understand but felt deep in his bones.

As they pulled into the driveway and he helped her inside, he kissed her forehead softly. "I'll take care of everything. Just rest."

Marica smiled weakly, but Edward could see the confusion in her eyes, the unease in the way she held herself. She didn't know either. But as she rested on the couch, a small, quiet voice inside her began to wonder if, perhaps, it wasn't just the exhaustion. Could it be something more? Something that would change everything?

The next day, after a restless night of mixed emotions, Marica found herself sitting nervously in the sterile white room of the doctor's office. The sound of the clock ticking on the wall felt louder than usual, a constant reminder of the weight of the moment.

She had chosen to go alone, not wanting to add to Edward's stress with his work at the restaurant. She told herself she could manage on her own, after all, she had always been independent. But today... Today, everything felt different.

Her mind raced, spinning in circles of uncertainty. Could this really be happening? The test, the nausea, the fainting spells... It was all leading up to this moment, but she still couldn't believe it.

The doctor entered, a warm smile on her face, but Marica couldn't quite meet her eyes. Her hands fidgeted in her lap, her heart pounding in her chest. The doctor ran through the usual questions, asking about her symptoms, her health, her history. And then, the moment came.

With a gentle look, the doctor turned to Marica, her voice soft but clear. "Marica, congratulations. You're pregnant."

Tears welled up in Marica's eyes, catching her by surprise. The world around her blurred as the news hit her, an overwhelming rush of emotions. She wasn't prepared for this. She hadn't thought through what it would feel like. Her heartbeat thundered in her ears, drowning out everything else.

Marica's hands trembled slightly as she gripped the edge of the chair. The tears spilled over, unbidden. She wasn't sure if it was joy, fear, or the sheer weight of it all. The room felt smaller, the air thick, as if the news had altered the very space she occupied.

She wanted to tell Edward so badly. Wanted to share this miracle with him in a way that would make it unforgettable. But there was a part of her that needed to hold on to it just a little longer, to savour this moment for herself before it became part of their shared story.

After she left the doctor's office, Marica took a deep breath, the weight of the secret heavy in her chest. She knew she had to find the right moment, a peaceful place, somewhere beautiful, to share this news with Edward. She couldn't just tell him any old way, this was too important, too precious.

Later that afternoon, after Edward finished working from his shift, she suggested a drive through the countryside, wanting to take a moment to breathe and reflect before telling him. Edward, as always, was up for the adventure, and they set off, winding along country lanes, the landscape unfolding before them. The fields rolled out like a vast green quilt, dotted with grazing sheep and wildflowers swaying gently in the breeze. The crisp autumn air carried the scent of earth and salt from the sea, mixing with the warmth of the sun on their skin.

They arrived at Trebah Garden, a place that had always filled Marica with a sense of calm. The lush subtropical paradise was a haven of peace, the air thick with the scent of ferns and damp earth. Towering trees and exotic plants flourished in the Cornish climate, their vibrant colours reflecting the golden hues of the morning light. The sound of a distant waterfall filled the air, and a small wooden bridge arched over a pond, its surface dotted with floating lilies.

As they walked through the garden, the peaceful sounds of birds and rustling leaves wrapped around them. Marica's steps slowed as they reached a secluded spot by the pond, where the water mirrored the deep blue of the sky above. She stood there for a moment, taking in the beauty of it all, feeling her heart race.

Turning to Edward, she took his hand in hers and gently placed his palm on her stomach. She smiled through the tears that were still threatening to fall, her voice soft but steady.

"What is it?" he asked, his brow furrowing in curiosity as he looked at her, sensing something was different.

Marica met his gaze, her eyes shining with a mix of wonder and joy. "We're going to be parents, Edward."

The words hung in the air between them, a new beginning, a new chapter. And in that moment, with the quiet of the garden surrounding them, it felt like time itself had paused, just for a heartbeat, to let the reality sink in.

"Are you serious?" Edward whispers, his voice thick with emotion.

She nods, and before she can say anything more, he sweeps her into his arms, lifting her off the ground. They spin together in the crisp afternoon air, laughter and tears mixing as golden leaves swirl around them like confetti.

"This is everything we've dreamed of," he murmurs against her hair.

In the quiet stillness of the garden, surrounded by nature's beauty, they hold each other close, knowing that everything they've ever wanted is just beginning.

Marica laughs, her heart soaring. The world feels like it's frozen, just for them. "I know," she whispers, her voice barely above a breath, tears filling her eyes. "I can't wait to meet our little one."

Edward spins her around again, his joy infectious, and Marica's heart bursts with love. This moment, this pure connection, is everything. She feels like the luckiest woman alive. He gently sets her down, his hands lingering on her shoulders, his gaze holding hers, filled with the same excitement, the same awe.

"We're doing this together," he says softly, his voice steady but full of wonder. "I'm going to be the best father I can be. For you. For our baby. I promise."

Marica smiles through her tears, her fingers brushing against his cheek. "I know you will, Edward. And I'll be right here with you. Always."

As the weeks pass, the excitement of their pregnancy fills their home. The once quiet cottage now hums with life. The living room is scattered with baby books, the nursery slowly taking shape with soft pastel colours, and tiny shoes waiting on a shelf.

In the small moments, when Edward pulls her close for a good morning kiss or when they share a quiet dinner by the fire, Marica feels the weight of their love grow stronger. And in the larger moments, like shopping for baby supplies or welcoming Edward's family with open arms, she knows their lives are about to change forever.

Edward's family has just returned from their travels around Europe, and Marica can tell that they've been longing to meet her, especially Edward's mother, Diana, who wraps Marica in a hug that feels so familiar, as though they've known each other forever.

"I'm so happy you're here, Marica," Diana says as they prepare a traditional Cornish dish together in the kitchen. Her voice is kind, like the gentle rustling of leaves in the wind. "You're exactly what Edward needs. He's been different since meeting you. Happier. More at peace."

Marica looks down at the mixing bowl, the warmth of Diana's words wrapping around her like a blanket. She smiles, her heart full. "Thank you, Diana," she replies softly, her voice thick with emotion. "I'm just so grateful to be here with him. He makes everything feel right."

Diana smiles, squeezing her hand. "It's wonderful to see him so happy. He deserves this."

Later that evening, the cottage is filled with the smell of freshly baked Cornish pasties, their flaky golden crusts tempting Marica with their warmth and comfort. Edward watches her with a grin, clearly enjoying the moment.

"You'll love these," Edward says, his eyes sparkling. "It's a Cornish tradition."

Marica takes a bite, savouring the rich filling and buttery crust, feeling as if the very essence of Cornwall has found its way into her heart. She smiles, feeling at home.

Diana brings out fresh scones, golden and inviting, accompanied by clotted cream and strawberry jam. The sweetness of the scones blends perfectly with the richness of the cream, and Marica feels as though she's found a little piece of heaven.

As the laughter dies down and the fire crackles softly, Robert swirls his wine and leans back in his chair with a knowing smile. "You know," he begins, his gaze settling on Edward, "since we're celebrating, I think it's only right Marica hears one of my favourite stories about young Edward."

Edward groans, already shaking his head. "Dad, no. Not in front of Marica."

"Oh, absolutely in front of Marica," Diana chimes in, grinning. "She needs to know what she's signed up for."

Robert clears his throat dramatically. "So, picture this— Edward, age seven, determined to become a pirate."

Marica chuckles, glancing at Edward, who's rubbing his forehead. "A pirate?"

"A full-fledged, treasure-hunting, swashbuckling pirate," Robert confirms. "He even made himself a pirate flag out of an old bed sheet and raided the entire house looking for 'loot.'"

"I was very resourceful," Edward mutters.

"Oh, you were something, all right," Robert continues. "One day, he decided he needed a proper ship. So, what does he do? He takes his mother's best wooden laundry basket, ties it to the dog with his school tie, and sets sail across the backyard, shouting, 'Full speed ahead, Captain Biscuit!'"

Marica bursts into laughter. "No!"

"Yes!" Diana says, shaking her head. "Poor Biscuit was the most patient dog, but he was not prepared for a life at sea."

Robert grins. "The 'ship' made it about two feet before it capsized into a flower bed. Edward came out covered in mud, still shouting about treasure, while Biscuit ran for his life."

Edward sighs dramatically. "In my defence, I was a very ambitious child."

"And a very dirty one," Diana adds. "Took us an hour to scrub him clean."

Marica wipes tears of laughter from her eyes. "I can't believe you tried to turn your dog into a pirate crew."

Edward shrugs. "Every great captain needs a first mate."

Robert raises his glass. "To Captain Biscuit, the bravest of them all."

As the family erupts into laughter once more, Marica looks at Edward, her heart full. She can already imagine the stories they'll tell their own daughter one day.

"To Edward and Marica," Robert says, his gaze moving between his son and Marica. "May your life be filled with love, laughter, and endless happiness. Marriage is a journey, one filled with adventures, a few storms, and plenty of beautiful moments. But through it all, if you hold onto each other, you'll always find your way home. We're proud to welcome you to the family, Marica. Welcome home."

Marica smiles, her hand resting gently in Edward's. She feels the love in the room, in every word spoken, in every toast raised. But when Robert offers her the glass, she hesitates, then shakes her head slightly, a faint blush warming her cheeks.

"I'm sorry, I can't drink the wine," she says softly.

All eyes turn to her with quiet curiosity. Then, Marica glances at Edward, her smile growing. "Because we have some wonderful news to share, don't we, love?"

112

Edward's eyes light up with realization. He turns to his family, his voice steady yet brimming with excitement. "We're having a baby girl."

For a heartbeat, the room is silent. Then gasps and joyful laughter ripple through the air.

Diana's hands fly to her face, tears of joy shimmering in her eyes. "A baby girl? Oh, my darling, that's the most wonderful news! I'm so incredibly happy for both of you."

Robert rises from his seat, his face breaking into a proud, beaming smile. "A baby girl," he repeats, his voice thick with emotion. "That's something truly special."

Marica's heart swells as Edward's family embraces her, their warmth and excitement wrapping around her like a comforting embrace. In that moment, she realizes just how deeply she belongs here—with them, with Edward.

"Thank you," she whispers, her voice unsteady with emotion. "I never imagined I'd find a family like this. You've all made me feel so welcome. I'm truly blessed."

Edward takes her hand, his fingers warm and steady. He doesn't need to say anything, his eyes say it all.

This is home. As they sit together, surrounded by love and laughter, Marica knows that whatever challenges lie ahead, this love will be their foundation, a love so deep, so unshakable, that no storm could ever break it… or could it?

Chapter 18: The Tragic Accident

The storm raged on, rain hammering against the windshield as Edward gripped the steering wheel, his knuckles white. The wipers swiped furiously, but the world beyond the glass remained a blur of darkness and water. The road was slick, treacherous.

Yet, it wasn't just the storm that unsettled him.

It was Victor.

It had started with an unexpected call. An unscheduled meeting. At first, Edward assumed it was a last-minute briefing, such things weren't uncommon in his role with the Royal Air Force. But as soon as he stepped into the dimly lit café on the outskirts of town, he knew this wasn't official business.

Victor was already there, seated in the corner, fingers wrapped around a glass of whiskey. He was the kind of man who moved through life with dangerous ease.

Edward didn't bother with pleasantries. "What the hell are you doing here?"

Victor smirked. "Still as direct as ever. Have a seat."

Edward remained standing. "I don't have time for this."

Victor let out a slow, exaggerated sigh. "That's a shame… because whether you like it or not, we need to talk."

Edward's patience thinned. "I'm RAF. Whatever mess you're tangled in, I want no part of it."

Victor tilted his head, amusement flickering in his eyes. "Oh, Ed… you say that as if we're strangers. Or have you forgotten the debts you owed before you put on that uniform?"

Edward's jaw tightened. "That was a lifetime ago."

Victor reached into his jacket. Edward tensed, instinctively ready for the worst, but all Victor pulled out was a folded piece of paper. He slid it across the table.

"Take a look."

Edward hesitated, pulse hammering in his ears. When he finally unfolded it, his breath caught.

It was an address. His address.

Marica.

His fists clenched. "Stay the hell away from my wife."

Victor leaned back, unbothered. "That depends on you, mate. Do what I ask, and she stays safe. Ignore me, and, well… accidents happen."

Edward forced himself to stay composed. "You don't scare me."

Victor smirked. "That's your problem, Ed. You should be scared."

Edward shoved the paper back at him. "I don't owe you anything."

Victor straightened his jacket as he stood. "Then I guess we'll see how this plays out." A knowing look, a slow nod, and then he was gone, vanishing into the night as easily as he had come.

Now, speeding down the rain-slicked road, the weight of that meeting pressed against Edward's chest.

His phone vibrated in the console beside him. An unknown number. He let it ring.

The rain drummed against the windshield like a warning. His pulse was a steady drum in his ears. Victor's voice echoed in his mind. Marica's address.

He needed to get home. Needed to warn her.

Then, in the rearview mirror—

Headlights.

A car. Dark. Sleek. Too close.

His gut twisted. It wasn't a coincidence.

He changed lanes. The car followed.

His phone buzzed again. A text.

"Told you accidents happen."

A cold wave of adrenaline surged through him.

Then—bam!

The force sent him lurching forward, the seatbelt biting into his chest. His tires shrieked against the wet pavement as he fought to steady the wheel.

Another hit. Harder this time.

The impact jerked the car sideways, the rear fishtailing wildly. Edward gritted his teeth, trying to regain control. But the rain had turned the road into glass, and the tires struggled for traction.

He glanced in the mirror. The sedan loomed behind him like a predator, its headlights cutting through the storm.

This wasn't just intimidation. This was a kill shot.

Not tonight.

He slammed his foot on the gas. The engine roared in protest. If they wanted a chase, they'd get one.

The road ahead curved sharply, a narrow stretch flanked by dense trees and an unforgiving metal barrier. He took the turn fast, the tires skidding dangerously close to the edge.

The sedan followed. No hesitation.

Edward scanned the road. There. A break in the trees just past the next bend. A service road, barely visible through the downpour. It was a long shot, but it was all he had.

He veered off the main road. Tires splashed through puddles, mud kicking up as he maneuvered the winding path. The sedan hesitated for only a second before following.

His breath came fast. If he could just—

Another hit. Straight to the side.

The jolt sent him careening toward the embankment. The car teetered, fighting against the slick ground.

Almost there. Almost—

A final, brutal slam.

The world flipped.

Metal groaned. Glass shattered. The sky and ground blurred into one.

Edward barely had time to register the impact before everything went black.

And in that last fleeting second before oblivion, one name tore through his mind.

Marica.

Chapter 19: A Life Hanging in the Balance

The piercing wail of sirens cut through the night as paramedics worked quickly to extract Edward from the wreckage. His RAF identification card was barely visible beneath the shattered glass and blood stained uniform. His pulse was weak but present.

At Royal Cornwall Hospital in Truro, Marica stood frozen in the sterile white hallway, her heart pounding as the doctor approached.

"Mrs. Carter?"

She barely found her voice. "Yes… I'm Marica Carter."

The doctor's expression was solemn. "Your husband was in a severe accident. He sustained multiple fractures, internal bleeding, and a head injury. We've stabilized him for now, but…" He hesitated. "His condition is critical."

Marica swayed, gripping the wall for support. "Will he wake up?"

The doctor sighed. "We don't know yet."

Her breath hitched.

She forced herself to push through the fear. "Can I see him?"

The doctor nodded. "Just for a moment."

As she stepped inside the dimly lit ICU room, the sight of Edward nearly broke her. The strong, confident man she had married, the man who held her like she was his entire world, now lay helpless, surrounded by machines keeping him alive.

She approached cautiously, brushing a trembling hand over his bruised face.

"Edward," she whispered, voice breaking. "I need you to wake up. I need you to come back to me."

Tears streamed down her cheeks. "I don't care what happened. Just wake up."

But he didn't stir.

Days passed. Edward remained unconscious. Marica refused to leave his side.

One night, unable to sleep, she decided to gather some fresh clothes from home. As she searched his drawers, something unexpected caught her eye, a journal she had never seen before.

Her fingers hesitated before opening it.

At first, the entries were normal, his thoughts on deployments, memories of their wedding, little notes about how much he loved her. But then towards the end his handwriting grew urgent.

"Victor found me. I don't know how, but he did. He knows about Marica. I need to protect her. I need to end this before it's too late."

Marica's blood ran cold.

Victor. The name haunted her.

Flipping through the pages, she uncovered the truth, Edward had a past she never knew about. A debt. A dangerous connection. A deal that had gone horribly wrong.

And then, in one of the last entries:

"If anything happens to me, it wasn't an accident."

Her hands shook. Edward's crash…It wasn't an accident. It was an attack.

A deliberate attempt to silence him.

Marica clutched the journal to her chest, her heart hammering.

She had to find out the truth.

Before it was too late.

Chapter 20: A Call in the Dark

Marica sat beside Edward, clutching his cold hand, her mind racing. The words from his journal haunted her.

If anything happens to me, it wasn't an accident.

She had to know the truth.

Edward's military background meant he was always cautious, so how had Victor managed to get to him? And what exactly did he want?

She wasn't going to sit back and wait for answers. She needed to act.

Marica traced Edward's last known movements. Before the accident, he had attended an official RAF dinner but had taken an unusual detour afterward. His phone records showed a call made just before the crash… to an unknown number.

With a deep breath, she dialled it.

It rang once.

Twice.

A click. Then silence.

She almost hung up until a deep, gravelly voice spoke.

"So, you finally found me."

Marica's heart pounded. "Victor."

A low chuckle. "I was wondering when you'd call."

Her grip tightened on the phone. "I know what you did."

Victor sighed dramatically. "Marica, Marica... You're smart. But you don't know the whole story. Edward owes me."

"He doesn't owe you anything!" she snapped.

"Oh, but he does." His tone darkened. "And now... you do too."

A chill ran down her spine.

Victor continued, "Your husband made a deal long before you came into his life. He thought he could escape it. Thought the Air Force would protect him. But debts don't just vanish."

Marica clenched her jaw. "If you hurt him—"

"I didn't have to," Victor cut in. "I only needed to remind him that running was useless. He was in a hurry that night, wasn't he? Look what happened."

Her blood boiled. *He forced Edward into that crash.*

She took a shaky breath. "What do you want?"

Victor chuckled. "Smart girl."

Then his voice dropped to a whisper.

"Meet me. If you want the truth."

A location followed. *The abandoned tin mine at Botallack, on the cliffs of Cornwall.*

He hung up.

Marica stared at the phone.

Her entire body screamed at her not to go.

But she had to.

For Edward.

Chapter 21: The Edge of Truth

The wind curled around Marica as she pulled her coat tighter, the chill sinking into her bones. The cliffs of Botallack stretched before her, dark and unforgiving, the waves crashing violently against the jagged rocks below. The ruins of an old tin mine stood like ghosts of the past, their broken walls whispering secrets to the wind.

She had never been here before.

Edward had, though.

She could almost hear his voice, rich with that quiet confidence he always carried. *"It's wild, untamed. Feels like the edge of the world."*

And now, here she was—standing at the edge, feeling like she was about to fall.

A flicker of light caught her eye. The glow of a cigarette, faint against the darkness.

Victor.

He leaned against a rusted railing, the wind whipping his coat around him. His posture was casual, but there was something dangerous in the way he held himself, like a man who had all the time in the world.

She stepped forward, her heartbeat drumming in her ears. "I'm here."

A slow smile tugged at the corner of his mouth as he flicked the cigarette away. "I never doubted you'd come."

Marica kept her distance. "Tell me what you want."

Victor studied her for a long moment before he sighed, shaking his head. "You always did have a fire in you, didn't you?" He reached into his coat and pulled out an envelope, letting it dangle between his fingers. "Your husband wasn't in that crash by accident."

Her breath hitched, but she forced herself to stay calm. "I know."

Victor's smirk widened. "Do you? Or do you just want to believe you do?"

She clenched her jaw. "Edward wasn't a liar."

Victor chuckled, low and knowing. "Oh, Marica… we both know that's not true."

Her fingers curled into fists. "You're lying."

He took a slow step toward her, holding out the envelope. "See for yourself."

She hesitated before snatching it from his hands. The paper was damp from the sea air, the ink smudged in places. She flipped through it, her pulse pounding.

Letters. Bank statements. Contracts.

Her name was on one of them.

A loan. One she had never signed.

Her heart squeezed painfully in her chest. "What is this?"

Victor exhaled, watching her carefully. "Your husband made a deal. A desperate one. He owed money to the wrong people. He borrowed it to cover up something that could've destroyed him."

She shook her head, her mind reeling. "No. He wouldn't—"

"He would," Victor interrupted. "And he did." He motioned to the papers. "A missing weapons shipment. Money transferred to the wrong hands. He was trying to fix a mistake before anyone found out."

Marica felt the weight of it pressing down on her.

Edward had been keeping secrets.

And now, she was tangled in them.

Victor took a step back, his voice softer now, almost pitying. "He thought he could outrun it. He thought the Air Force would protect him. But debts like his don't just disappear, Marica."

She met his gaze, her voice barely above a whisper. "What do you want from me?"

Victor smiled, slow and deliberate. "Your loyalty."

Her stomach clenched.

She had always believed in Edward, in their love, in the life they had built. But now, standing on the edge of the cliffs, with the truth unravelling around her, she realised—

The man she loved had been hiding something far more dangerous than she'd ever imagined.

And now, it was her burden to carry.

Marica stood there, holding the envelope in her hand, her mind racing. The wind howled around her, but it felt like the world had gone silent. She could barely process the words Victor had spoken, the cold reality settling like a heavy stone in her chest.

That was what he wanted. But loyalty to whom? To Edward, the man she thought she knew completely, or to Victor, the man who had nearly destroyed him?

She swallowed hard, trying to steady herself. "Loyalty?" Her voice was steady, but beneath it lay a tremor of disbelief. "What do you mean by that?"

Victor's gaze remained fixed on her, his eyes cold and calculating. He had no empathy, no remorse for what he had put them through. "Edward's not the only one who's in debt now. You and I both know what he's left behind. If you want to keep him safe, if you want to stop this from becoming more than just a car crash... You'll help me. You'll keep this quiet."

Her hands trembled, the cold air making it worse. "What are you threatening? What do you want from me?"

He took a step closer, closing the distance between them. "Edward's debts are far from over. If he recovers, and I have no reason to believe that he won't, he's going to have to answer

128

for what he did. But if he can't—" Victor paused, letting the implication hang in the air like a bitter wind, "—then it's on you, Marica. You'll be the one to manage the consequences."

Her heart hammered in her chest as the truth hit her like a punch to the gut. Victor didn't care about Edward; he was using him as leverage. The debts, the secrets, none of it mattered to him beyond his own gain.

"Why me?" she whispered, the words raw in her throat.

Victor gave a slight shrug, the smugness never leaving his face. "Because you're his weakness. You were always his weakness.

You're the one thing that could make him do anything. You're the one thing that can make him bend to my will."

Marica's hands clenched tighter around the envelope, and for a fleeting moment, she wanted to throw it at his face, to make him feel the weight of all the lies, the betrayal. But she knew that wouldn't solve anything.

She looked at Victor, her voice growing cold and measured. "You think I'll just turn my back on everything I've built with Edward, for you?"

Victor's smile deepened, but there was no warmth in it. "No. I don't think so. I think you'll do whatever it takes to protect him. Because you love him. And I know exactly how to use that against you."

The words cut through her like a knife. She had always prided herself on the love she and Edward shared, on how they had built something real together, despite their pasts. But now, as

129

she stood there, facing the dark side of his secrets, she was torn between the man she loved and the fear that everything she had believed in might be a lie.

"I won't be a part of this," she said, her voice steady but her heart racing. "I will not help you."

Victor's eyes narrowed. "You don't have a choice."

Marica met his gaze, trying to hold onto the strength that had always been her anchor. "I do have a choice. I'm not afraid of you."

The cold breeze whipped around them again, but this time, Marica's hands were steady. She felt the weight of the envelope still in her grip, the secrets inside now a burden she wasn't sure how to carry. But she knew one thing for certain, Victor was trying to break her, trying to make her choose between the man she loved and the truth.

And for the first time, Marica wasn't sure where she stood anymore.

Victor's expression darkened, but he didn't push any further. Instead, he simply nodded, as though this conversation had already played out in his mind.

"Then you'll see soon enough," he said, turning to walk away. "When Edward wakes up... when he's forced to face what he's done, we'll see what kind of loyalty you really have. I'll be waiting, Marica. We all have our debts to pay."

His footsteps faded into the night, leaving Marica standing alone on the cliffs, the sea crashing violently beneath her.

She was left with the envelope, the truth about Edward's past, and the horrifying realisation that her world was changing, shifting, and she was caught in the middle of it.

As she watched Victor disappear into the darkness, she clenched her jaw. *She wouldn't let him win. She wouldn't let Edward's past define their future.* But the battle was far from over.

The next morning, as the sun crept over the horizon, Marica found herself sitting at Edward's bedside again, her thoughts swirling. She had not slept, not really. Every time she closed her eyes, Victor's words echoed in her mind. She couldn't just keep pretending everything was okay. The man she loved was tangled in a web of secrets and debts, and the truth was something she could no longer ignore.

When Edward finally stirred, his fingers twitching, Marica was there, waiting. His eyes fluttered open, weak and confused, but when he saw her, he seemed to focus for a moment.

"Marica," he whispered, his voice hoarse. "You... you're here…"

She took his hand, her heart aching. "I'm here, Edward. I'm not going anywhere."

But in the pit of her stomach, she wondered if things would ever be the same again. Would Edward be the man he once was? Could they rebuild the life they had, or was this the beginning of the end for them?

There was so much she still didn't know, and for the first time, she wasn't sure she could trust the man she'd pledged to spend her life with.

But one thing was certain—she wasn't giving up on him yet.

Not without a fight.

Chapter 22: Unravelling the Past

Edward's breathing was shallow, but his eyes remained fixed on Marica as he tried to process the warmth of her hand in his. His voice was barely a whisper. "Marica... what happened?"

Her heart clenched, but she kept her gaze steady. "You were in an accident, Edward. A serious one." She took a deep breath, swallowing the urge to say everything that was tumbling through her mind, everything she was still too afraid to face. "But you're going to be okay. You're going to recover."

Edward blinked slowly, his face scrunching as he tried to remember. "I... don't remember much." His voice faltered. "What about the crash? What happened?"

Marica hesitated, unsure how to answer. She wanted to shield him, to keep him from the terrible truths that were swirling around them. But she knew she couldn't do that anymore. Not with Victor's words hanging over her like a dark cloud. Not with the nagging feeling in her gut telling her that nothing would ever be the same again.

"I'm not sure, Edward." She hesitated, her gaze dropping to their entwined hands. "But I don't think it was just an accident. Someone's behind this. And I believe it's connected to your past... something you haven't told me."

Edward's eyes fluttered closed, his face pale with exhaustion. "My past..." he whispered.

He seemed to struggle for words. "There's a lot I should have told you, Marica. A lot I should have said."

Marica squeezed his hand tighter. "You can tell me now. Please, Edward. I need to know what's going on. I need to know why this is happening."

He winced, the weight of her words clearly sinking in. Slowly, he turned his head, meeting her eyes with a look that carried more guilt than she'd ever seen in him before.

"I didn't want you to know. I didn't want you to have to carry this burden too. But there's no escaping it now, is there?" He sighed heavily. "The debts… they're not just financial. They're personal. And Victor… he's not just some business partner. He's someone I made a deal with years ago—before you and I even met."

Marica's breath caught. "A deal? What kind of deal, Edward?"

He swallowed hard, as if the words were physically painful to speak. "It was a loan—no, not just a loan. A life-altering agreement. I thought I could get away from it. That my time in the Air Force would protect me, but I was wrong. Victor's been coming for me, waiting for me to slip up."

Marica's mind raced, trying to piece together the fragments of what he was telling her. "But why? Why would you do something like that? You never said anything."

Edward turned his head away, looking out the window as though searching for an answer in the sky. "I didn't have a choice. At the time, I thought it was the only way I could protect my family. But it wasn't just about money. It was about loyalty, and that's something I didn't realize I was risking until now." He paused, his voice barely above a whisper. "Loyalty to the wrong person."

Marica felt a cold wave wash over her as the realisation began to settle in. "Victor is dangerous, isn't he?"

Edward closed his eyes, his expression grim. "More dangerous than you can imagine. He's not a man you can just walk away from. And I have learned that the hard way."

Marica swallowed, feeling her chest tighten. "What do we do now? What do you want me to do, Edward?"

Edward reached for her hand weakly, his fingers brushing hers in a plea for reassurance. "You need to stay out of this, Marica. It's too dangerous. You don't understand the lengths he's willing to go to. He'll hurt anyone to get what he wants."

She shook her head, the sting of his words burning through her. "I'm not going to leave you, Edward. Not now. Not after everything we've been through."

He looked up at her, his eyes filled with both fear and love. "I don't want to put you in danger. You don't deserve this."

Marica's throat tightened. "We're in this together, Edward. If we're going to figure this out, we do it as a team. We fight back together."

Edward's expression softened for a moment, but then the heaviness returned. "Victor won't stop. He'll come after us until the debt is paid. He thinks he owns me, Marica. And now, he thinks he owns you too."

Marica shook her head resolutely. "No. I refuse to be a pawn in his game. I'll do whatever it takes to protect you—and to stop him from destroying everything we've built."

She stood up, her mind already racing with plans. "I'll find a way to take him down. I don't care what it costs."

Edward's eyes widened. "Marica—"

She pressed her finger to his lips, silencing him. "We've already lost so much, Edward. But we still have a chance to fight back. And I'm not going to sit here and wait for him to come for us again."

Edward watched her, his eyes full of both admiration and fear. "I never wanted this for you, Marica. I never wanted to drag you into my mess."

She gave him a small, determined smile. "You didn't. But this is our mess now. And we're going to fix it—together."

As she left the room, Marica felt a wave of determination course through her. There was so much to uncover, so many truths still hidden beneath layers of deceit and betrayal. But one thing was clear: she wasn't going to let Victor destroy their lives. Not without a fight. Not while there was still breath in her body.

Chapter 23: The Depths of Deceit

Marica stood in the quiet of the hallway, her pulse racing in her ears. Every word Edward had spoken echoed in her mind, a constant drumbeat of realisation and fear. Victor, the name alone sent a chill through her. And yet, the man had been more than just a shadow in their lives. He was a ghost, lurking in the background, manipulating, controlling, and waiting for the perfect moment to strike.

She took a deep breath, steadying herself. There was no turning back now. Edward's past, the debts he'd tried to outrun, the promises he had made to someone like Victor, it was all coming to light. The truth was heavier than she could have ever imagined, and the stakes had never been higher.

But it wasn't just about Edward anymore. Victor's reach extended far beyond him. It had touched her life, entwining their fates in a twisted dance neither of them had asked for.

Marica needed answers. She needed to know why this was happening, and most importantly, how she could stop it before it consumed them both.

Her thoughts raced as she moved swiftly down the hallway, her footsteps echoing off the walls. She had to find out everything she could about Victor, his connections, his past, his business dealings. Whatever it took, she would unravel the truth. And with it, she would find a way to destroy the grip he had on their lives.

That night, as Marica sat alone in the dim light of their cottage, the weight of the situation was nearly suffocating. She had just returned from the hospital, where Edward had been resting after a restless afternoon. He had insisted on trying to get up, to act as though nothing had changed, but the exhaustion in his eyes spoke volumes. They both knew it would take more than time for him to recover from the trauma, both physical and emotional.

But it wasn't just Edward who was broken. She was too, broken by the secrets, by the lies, and by the fear that had settled so deeply inside her. She couldn't keep running away from the truth any longer. The life they had built was being threatened by forces far stronger than her love for Edward. And the reality was, she was just as vulnerable as he was.

She leaned over the table, sifting through papers, old emails, and anything she could find that might provide even the slightest clue about Victor's past dealings. Her fingers trembled as she opened an old, nondescript folder she had discovered hidden in a drawer. Inside, the first page was a list of names, none of them familiar—except one. The last name on the list was underlined twice.

Victor D'Amato.

Marica's heart skipped a beat. Her instincts flared. There it was. She had found something—something that might unlock everything. The rest of the document was filled with cryptic notes, references to meetings, locations, and dates.

But the most important detail was that Victor's name had been attached to these notes for years. Years longer than she had known Edward.

She sifted through the pages, looking for anything that might give her more insight into what Victor had planned, what his true intentions were. Her eyes landed on a handwritten note that made her stomach drop.

"Victor D'Amato will not stop until the debt is paid. Even if it means taking down anyone in his path."

The words were simple, but they carried the weight of a thousand unanswered questions. Who had written this? Why had they left this warning behind?

The cold dread that had been lingering in her chest suddenly spiked. She wasn't just fighting to save Edward. She was fighting for her own survival.

The morning was quiet, the kind of stillness that often preceded a storm. Marica stood by the window, watching the mist curl over the trees, a cup of tea growing cold in her hands. She had spent the last few days buried in research, trying to make sense of the puzzle that had become her life. But no amount of planning could prepare her for what came next.

Her phone rang, the sharp sound cutting through the silence. She frowned at the unknown number. A moment of hesitation. Then, slowly, she pressed *accept*.

"Hello?"

A deep, gravelly voice filled the line. *"Ms. Marica, this is Detective Thomas. I need to speak with you about a matter involving a man named Victor D'Amato."*

The name hit her like a gust of wind, knocking the air from her lungs.

"Victor D'Amato?" she repeated, gripping the phone tighter. Her voice was barely above a whisper, as if saying his name out loud might summon him.

"I think it's best we meet in person," the detective said, his tone steady, unwavering. *"I've been investigating D'Amato for a long time. He's not who he claims to be. And I believe you might be in danger."*

The line went dead.

For a moment, Marica couldn't move. The room around her felt suddenly too small, the walls pressing in. She had known— *deep down, she had known*—that something wasn't right. But hearing it spoken aloud, hearing confirmation from someone who had been following Victor's trail, made it feel terrifyingly real.

She wasn't just caught in the crossfire. She was *part* of whatever this was.

What she didn't know was that Detective Thomas had been investigating Victor D'Amato for months, uncovering a trail of criminal activity that spanned multiple cities, extortion, fraud, and unexplained disappearances.

His latest findings led him to Edward, a man with past ties to D'Amato. Digging deeper, Thomas discovered Edward's connection to Marica. Recent surveillance footage, flagged police reports, and intercepted communications suggested she wasn't just an innocent bystander, she was a potential target. Concerned for her safety, he pulled her contact details from law enforcement databases and made the call.

Somewhere far away, a clock chimed.

Marica exhaled slowly, pressing a hand to her chest, trying to still the frantic rhythm of her heart. But there was no time for fear. No time for second-guessing. If there were answers to be found, she needed them *now.*

She grabbed her coat and stepped outside, the crisp air biting against her skin. The weight of uncertainty clung to her, but she squared her shoulders and kept walking. Because whatever lay ahead, whatever secrets this detective held, she was ready to face them.

The detective's office was tucked away in a quiet corner of Saint Ives, far from the hustle and bustle of the town's cobblestone streets. The space felt like a relic, untouched by time, dimly lit, with the scent of worn leather and old paper in the air. Marica hesitated at the doorway before stepping inside, the weight of the moment pressing down on her.

Detective Thomas was a man shaped by years of quiet observation and unspoken truths. His eyes were sharp, like someone who'd seen more than he cared to, and his posture spoke of a life spent in shadows.

He watched her closely as she entered, then motioned for her to sit. Without a word, he poured two cups of coffee and slid one toward her.

"You're here because of Victor," he said, his voice low, controlled. *"And if I'm right, you're closer to him than you realize."*

A cold shiver ran down Marica's spine. She wrapped her hands around the warm cup, trying to steady her breath. *"What do you know about him? About his dealings?"*

The detective leaned forward, his fingers entwining on the desk. *"I've been tracking him for years. He's not just some small-time con man. He moves between towns, leaving chaos in his wake. But recently, I discovered something much larger, a dangerous syndicate he's tied to. They don't just break the law. They control it. And Victor? He's one of their key players."*

Her heart raced in her chest. A *syndicate?* The weight of his words hung heavily in the air.

"How does this connect to Edward?" Marica asked, her voice barely steady.

The detective's gaze grew darker, more intense. *"Edward made a dangerous deal with Victor. And it's not just about money or debts. The people Victor works for—well, they don't take your money. They take everything."*

Marica's world tilted. She had spent so long trying to piece together the fragments of Edward's past, trying to understand him. But this—this was something far beyond what she had ever imagined.

The detective stood, moving to a worn filing cabinet at the side of the room. He retrieved a thick folder and placed it gently in front of her, though he didn't open it. *"There's more, but I can't share it all right now. Just know this: Victor isn't someone you can afford to underestimate. He'll stop at nothing to get what he wants."*

142

Marica's breath hitched, but something deep inside her hardened. She had spent far too long running from the truth, from the shadows that clung to Edward's past. It was time to face it.

Victor wouldn't win. Not now. Not ever.

Chapter 24: The Final Betrayal

Marica sat in the detective's office long after he had finished speaking, the weight of his words pressing down on her chest. Her mind spun with the new truths she had learned. Edward, the man she loved, had been tangled in a world she never could have imagined, a world that wasn't just about betrayal but also about loss, regret, and things far beyond her understanding. But what terrified her even more than that was the reality that this world wasn't over. It was still out there, lurking, threatening to pull them both into its depths.

Victor wasn't just a name. He was a shadow, a reminder of the past that Edward couldn't escape, no matter how hard he tried. And Marica knew, no matter how much she wished for things to be different, that the past always had a way of finding its way to the present.

"You need to be careful, Marica," the detective had warned, his voice steady but full of a kind of wisdom borne from years of quiet pain. "Victor's reach is vast. And you don't know who you can trust—not even the people closest to you."

She had nodded then, but now, those words echoed in her mind, chilling her to the core. *Trust no one.* It sounded simple enough, but it was a lesson that cut deeper than she could have imagined. She thought of Rachel, the woman who had been like a sister to her, who had shared quiet moments with her through the years, never once hinting at the secrets she might be keeping.

Her phone buzzed as she stepped out of the detective's office, the number unfamiliar. When she answered, she heard Edward's voice, worn but familiar.

"Marica," he said, his voice rough, as though he'd been carrying something heavy for too long. "I need to talk to you."

The relief of hearing his voice was short-lived. "Edward? What is it?" she asked, but her stomach twisted in anticipation.

"I think... I think Victor has someone on the inside," he said, the words barely more than a whisper, but they struck her like a blow. "Someone close to us."

A cold chill gripped her. "What do you mean? Who?" she asked, her heart pounding.

"I don't know yet," he said, his voice filled with an uncertainty that Marica had never heard before. "But I'm starting to think someone I trusted, someone I thought had my back, has been feeding Victor information. About me. About us."

Marica closed her eyes, the weight of his words sinking in. She couldn't process it. Not yet. Not Rachel. *Not Rachel.* The idea was too much, too painful to even consider.

"I'll be there soon," she said, her voice a steady lie, masking the panic she felt rising in her chest. "We'll figure this out. Together."

As she ended the call, Marica's heart sank. Betrayal was a bitter pill to swallow, but it was even worse when it came from someone you thought was family. And for a moment, just a moment, she wondered if there was any hope left for them at all.

When she arrived back at their cottage, nestled in the quiet of Saint Ives, Edward was sitting on the couch, the space around him eerily still. He had just come home from the hospital, and though he tried to mask the exhaustion in his eyes, it was clear that the toll of the past few weeks had worn him thin. The familiar scent of pine from the trees outside mingled with the smell of fresh coffee brewing in the kitchen, a contrast to the storm swirling in Marica's chest.

He looked up as she entered, his gaze carrying a kind of quiet strength, but also a vulnerability she hadn't seen before. He had always been her rock, her protector. But now, in the dim light of their cottage, he seemed smaller somehow, worn down by the weight of their shared struggle.

"Marica," he said, his voice low, his expression grim. "I think I know who it is."

"Who?" she whispered, bracing herself.

"Rachel," he said, the name hanging in the air like a curse.

Rachel. The words barely made sense. Rachel, who had shared so many laughs with them, so many secrets.

Rachel, who had been there through the good times and the bad. It didn't make sense. But the doubt in Edward's eyes told her that it did.

Marica felt a lump form in her throat. "But... no, it can't be her."

Edward shook his head, his gaze steady but filled with regret. "I didn't want to believe it either. But it's too perfect. She's always there when we need her. Too much so. And I'm afraid... I'm afraid we've been blind all this time."

146

Tears threatened to blur her vision, but Marica fought them back. She couldn't break down now, not when everything they had fought for was on the line.

"We need to be sure," she said, her voice a quiet promise. "We can't let this tear us apart."

They didn't speak much after that, the weight of the truth settling over them like a shadow. Marica knew what had to be done. She had to confront Rachel. But more than that, she had to confront the fear that had always lurked in the corners of her mind, the fear that love wasn't always enough, and that sometimes, even the ones you loved the most could betray you in the worst way.

But as she looked at Edward, she knew she couldn't let this be the end. They had come too far together. And if there was any hope left, she would fight for it—for them—no matter what.

Chapter 25: Confronting Rachel

The dim light of the evening stretched long across the garden as Marica stood at the edge of the patio, her hands trembling as she stared out into the horizon. The sun had just dipped beneath the trees, leaving behind a soft glow that made everything feel surreal, as if the world was holding its breath. The peaceful silence of the cottage's surroundings felt like a cruel contrast to the storm brewing inside her heart.

Behind her, the door creaked open. Edward's voice, barely above a whisper, broke the silence. "Marica, are you sure you're ready for this?"

She didn't answer immediately. Instead, she closed her eyes, taking a slow, steady breath, as if trying to calm the whirlwind of emotions swirling within her. The weight of what lay ahead was suffocating, but it was nothing compared to the weight of the unknown. Victor—that name still sent a chill down her spine. But Rachel—Rachel's betrayal was a wound that Marica had yet to understand.

"I don't have a choice," she finally replied, her voice stronger than she felt. "Victor thinks he has us trapped, but we're not going to let him win."

Edward stepped closer, his presence warm and steady behind her. She could feel the comfort of his proximity, the silent promise of protection that he had always offered. He was her anchor in a sea of chaos.

"You don't have to do this alone," he said, his voice laced with quiet resolve, his hand brushing lightly against her back.

Marica turned to him, her gaze meeting his with a tenderness that made her heart ache. He was still the man she loved—the one who had stood by her side through every challenge. But this... this was different. The shadows of betrayal and danger hung between them like a veil, and no matter how hard she tried, she couldn't pretend they hadn't changed everything.

She wanted so much to believe that things could go back to the way they were before all of this started. Before Victor. Before the lies. Before Rachel. But deep down, she knew that wasn't possible. Not anymore.

"I can't just let it go, Edward," she said, her voice cracking with the weight of the truth. "I have to know what Rachel was hiding. I have to understand why she did this."

Edward's expression softened, but his eyes betrayed the understanding he had been trying to mask. His gaze dropped, and for a moment, the silence stretched between them like a living thing. The quiet wasn't comforting; it was heavy with the knowledge that there was no going back.

"Just promise me you'll be careful," he said, his voice low, filled with an undercurrent of concern. "Victor's a dangerous man, and so is she."

"I know," Marica whispered, her throat tight with emotion. "But I'm not going to stand by and watch him destroy everything we've worked for. Everything we've built."

Edward stepped closer, closing the distance between them, and for a moment, Marica felt the familiar warmth of his touch. She wanted to hold on to that warmth, to let it be a shield against the cold reality of their situation. But she knew she couldn't.

With a final glance at the fading light of the garden, Marica turned and walked back inside. She could hear the faint sound of Rachel's voice through the thin walls, and her pulse quickened. Rachel was here. In the cottage. Waiting.

The confrontation had been inevitable, but now that it was upon her, the weight of it felt overwhelming. She had to know the truth, the whole truth.

Marica walked toward the small room where Rachel was sitting, her figure tense but still as ever. The woman who had once been a friend, the woman whose secrets had been the catalyst for everything, was here.

And Marica was ready to confront her.

Chapter 26: The Final Showdown

The door to the small room creaked open, and Marica paused just inside the threshold, her breath catching as she took in the sight of Rachel. The dim light of the room cast long shadows over Rachel's figure, her back stiff, her hands folded neatly in her lap as though she were waiting for something, waiting for this very moment.

Rachel looked up slowly, her eyes meeting Marica's, and for a fleeting second, the old warmth Marica had once seen there seemed to flicker, before it was swallowed by something harder, colder. There was no apology, no remorse, only a cool detachment.

"Marica," Rachel said, her voice calm but tinged with something Marica couldn't quite place. "I knew you'd come."

Marica's heart thundered in her chest. The air between them was thick with years of unresolved tension, betrayal that had festered in the dark. She took a step forward, her voice cutting through the silence like a knife. "You knew? You knew what Victor was planning? All this time, you've been a part of it?"

Rachel's lips curled into something resembling a smile, but there was no humour in it. "It was never supposed to be like this. I never meant for it to get out of hand."

Marica's fists clenched at her sides, the weight of her emotions pressing down on her. The betrayal, the lies, everything Rachel had done, it was too much. Too much to forgive.

"You were supposed to be my friend, Rachel," Marica said, her voice trembling with barely contained fury. "You were supposed to be *on our side*."

Rachel's expression flickered for just a moment, but it was gone in the next heartbeat. She stood up from her chair, moving towards the small window and looking out into the gathering darkness. "I never meant to hurt you. I just… I wanted out. I wanted control, Marica. I was tired of being in the shadows, tired of always being the one who had to follow, who had to wait."

Marica's mind reeled. "You betrayed us all for *control*? For power? For what, Rachel? Was it worth it? Was any of it worth it?"

Rachel didn't answer immediately, and Marica felt her patience slipping away. She moved closer, her eyes narrowing. "Tell me the truth. What was Victor really after? Why did you help him?"

Rachel sighed, turning back to face Marica. Her face was pale, her eyes heavy with something that might have been regret, but it didn't matter now. The damage had already been done. "Victor always wanted more. More power, more influence. But he's smart, he doesn't go after things directly. He works through others. Through people like me. He used me to get closer to you, Marica. To destroy you. To destroy everything you've built with Edward."

Marica's stomach twisted. "And you let him? You helped him tear apart everything we fought for?"

Rachel's shoulders slumped, her voice softening. "I didn't see it that way at first. I thought I was just helping him get what he wanted. But then... then I saw what it was doing to you. To Edward. And I couldn't stop. It was too late."

Marica took a step back, her mind reeling. "So, what now, Rachel? You're telling me all this like it's some sort of confession, but it doesn't change anything. You can't just undo the damage you've done."

Rachel's face twisted in frustration. "I *never* wanted any of this. I made a mistake, Marica. A huge mistake. And now—" She stopped, swallowing hard as if struggling to find the words. "Now, I can't go back. But I can help you. If you'll let me."

Marica's eyes searched Rachel's face, looking for any trace of sincerity. The room felt smaller now, the walls closing in with the weight of everything Rachel had just said. Could she really trust her? Could she forgive the unforgivable?

"I don't know if I can forgive you, Rachel," Marica said, her voice low and steady. "But I can't do this alone. If you're really sorry, if you really want to make it right... help me stop Victor."

Rachel's gaze softened, and for the first time in what felt like forever, there was a hint of vulnerability in her eyes. "I will," she said quietly. "I'll do whatever it takes."

For a long moment, neither of them spoke. Marica stood there, torn between the desire to let go of the anger that had consumed her and the reality that Rachel's betrayal had already left scars too deep to heal easily.

Finally, Marica nodded. "I'm listening. But this has to end, Rachel. No more lies. No more games. We will finish this."

153

Rachel stepped forward, her face a mixture of determination and regret. "We finish this together."

As the words hung in the air, Marica felt a spark of something she hadn't felt in a long time—hope. It wasn't much, but it was enough to push her forward. They had a chance. Together, they might stand a chance against Victor and everything he represented.

And for the first time in what felt like forever, Marica believed that the truth—*the real truth*—was the key to their survival.

Chapter 27: Shattered Truths

The rain had started to fall heavily, tapping a rhythmic beat on the windows of the café as Marica sat across from Edward. The dim light cast shadows on the walls, and the weight of their conversation felt like it was pressing down on them both.

Edward's fingers drummed lightly on the table, a rhythm of impatience and concern. "So, Rachel... What exactly did she tell you?"

Marica sighed, rubbing her temples. "She's involved, Edward. She helped Victor. But she says she didn't know the extent of his plans. She didn't understand how far it would go." Her voice trailed off as doubt flickered within her. Could she believe Rachel? The betrayal stung too much to simply forgive. Yet, there was a part of her that wanted to believe in the possibility of redemption.

Edward leaned back, frustration clear on his face. "It's not that simple. Can we really trust her? After everything?"

Marica didn't have an answer, not yet. As much as she wanted to trust Rachel's words, she couldn't ignore the gnawing suspicion that lingered in her chest.

Before either of them could continue, the door to the café opened, and a tall figure stepped in, dripping wet from the rain. Marica immediately recognized him.

Detective Thomas.

His face was set in that familiar, determined expression, his eyes scanning the room until they landed on her. Without a word, he made his way to their table, pulling out the chair opposite them without asking.

"Detective," Edward greeted, his voice flat, wary.

"Marica," Thomas said, nodding slightly as he sat down. He didn't offer a greeting; he was all business. "We need to talk."

Marica felt a shiver run down her spine. "What is it, Detective?"

Thomas wasted no time. "I've been going through the information we've gathered on Victor. I've got people digging through his finances, his movements... And I think I've found something. Something that links him directly to a network I hadn't seen before."

Edward raised an eyebrow. "What network?"

Thomas leaned in closer, his voice lowering. "Victor's not just a lone player. There's an underground group—criminal, powerful people—who have been backing him. I've had suspicions for months, but now I've got the proof."

Marica's pulse quickened. "So, he's been playing a much bigger game than we realized."

"Exactly." Thomas's eyes narrowed. "This isn't just about us. It's about more than we can handle alone."

Marica's mind raced. If there was one thing she knew, it was that Victor's power had always been more than just money. It was an influence. But now, this? A network of criminals? It made her stomach churn.

Edward looked between the two of them, his frustration evident. "So, what do we do now?"

Thomas's gaze hardened. "We need to hit him where it hurts. I've been following the money trail, but the final piece of the puzzle is his next move. He's got something big planned, and if we can't stop him soon, we're going to be too late."

Marica leaned forward, her determination solidifying. "What do we need to do?"

Thomas studied her for a moment, as though weighing her words. "You've got connections to Rachel, right? She's in a position to help us. If she's really willing to turn on him, now's the time to use her. But you need to be careful. Trust her, but don't trust her completely."

Marica's breath caught in her throat. "I'm not sure I can trust her at all."

Edward put a hand on hers, his voice steady. "We don't have a choice. If Rachel can give us anything, it might be the only lead we have left."

Detective Thomas nodded, his eyes hardening. "I've got eyes on Victor's operations, but we need to move fast. This isn't just about revenge. It's about stopping him before he destroys everything."

The weight of the situation pressed down on Marica's chest, but she steeled herself. She had come too far to back down now.

"Alright," she said, her voice firm. "Let's do this. Whatever it takes."

Chapter 28: Tipping Point

The air inside the warehouse was thick with tension. Marica stood at the edge of the cavernous room, her hand resting on the cold metal of a nearby crate, her mind racing. The plan was in motion, but nothing felt certain. Detective Thomas had arranged everything, but she still didn't feel ready.

Rachel had agreed to cooperate—had promised to testify against Victor—but Marica couldn't shake the feeling that something was off. She had seen the way Rachel's eyes darted whenever she thought no one was looking, the tightness in her jaw. There was more to this than Rachel was letting on, and Marica wasn't sure if she was ready to uncover what that was.

Edward stood beside her, his presence a silent comfort. He wasn't saying much, but she could feel his quiet resolve. They both knew this was their chance to end it. The network that Victor had built, the power he had accumulated—it all came crashing down tonight. But only if they could pull it off.

"There's no turning back now," Edward said softly, his voice breaking the silence between them.

Marica nodded, her throat dry. "I know."

As if on cue, Detective Thomas entered the warehouse, his silhouette cutting through the dim light. He walked with purpose, his eyes scanning the room. He was accompanied by two of his officers, their presence a reminder that things were about to escalate.

"Everything's set," Thomas said, his voice low, eyes darting to the shadows. "Rachel's inside. We have enough evidence to tie Victor to the underground network, but we need to catch him in the act. We can't afford any mistakes."

Marica took a deep breath. "And if Rachel's lying? What then?"

Thomas looked at her for a long moment before answering. "We'll know soon enough. If she's playing us, we'll have enough backup to take her down with him."

The weight of his words settled over Marica. There was no more room for uncertainty. They had to move now.

The sound of footsteps echoed in the distance. Victor. He was close.

Edward squeezed her hand. "We're doing this together. We have each other. Always."

Marica gave him a small, uncertain smile. She wasn't sure if the words were for him or for herself. Either way, they both knew the stakes.

Moments later, the door to the warehouse creaked open. The figure standing in the doorway was unmistakable. **Victor**.

He was flanked by several of his men, all exuding that same cold confidence. But Marica saw something different in him now. The arrogance, the power, it was all starting to unravel. He wasn't as untouchable as he thought.

"Ah, Marica," Victor said, his voice dripping with mock amusement. "I knew you would come. You always were a fool for thinking you could stop me."

Marica met his gaze without flinching. "I'm done being your pawn, Victor. You're finished."

Victor's eyes narrowed, and for a brief moment, there was a flicker of something—fear, maybe? But it was quickly masked by his usual smirk. "You really think you've won?"

"I don't think," Marica said coldly. "I know."

The tense silence between them was broken by the sound of footsteps behind them. Rachel stepped into view, her face as pale as Marica had ever seen it. She wasn't looking at Marica or Victor; her eyes were on the ground, as if the weight of what she was about to do was too much for her to bear.

Victor turned toward her, his gaze darkening. "What's this? A change of heart?"

Rachel swallowed hard, her voice barely audible. "I'm done. I can't do this anymore. I can't be a part of your game."

Marica watched, her heart pounding, as Rachel stepped forward, her eyes now meeting hers. For the first time, Rachel looked vulnerable. "I didn't know, Marica. I swear I didn't know the extent of it. But I can't protect him anymore."

Victor's face twisted with rage. "You think you can betray me like this, Rachel? You think I won't—"

Chapter 29: The Struggle

The storm outside was relentless, its howling winds rattling the windows of the dimly lit room. The air inside felt thick, heavy with the kind of danger that seemed to press against the walls. Marica could barely breathe. Shadows stretched unnaturally, flickering across the floor like something from a nightmare.

Victor moved swiftly, almost too quickly. Edward didn't have time to react. Before anyone could process the moment, Victor had yanked open the desk drawer and pulled out a gun. The cold steel gleamed in the low light, and Marica's heart skipped a beat. She had left this life behind, or so she had thought.

"Marica," Victor's voice was a low growl, filled with menace. He grabbed her wrist with an iron grip, pulling her toward him. "Don't make me do this."

The barrel of the gun pressed cold against her temple, sending a shiver through her spine. She could hear the blood pounding in her ears, drowning out everything except for the danger that threatened to consume them.

"Let her go, Victor," Edward's voice cracked but remained steady. He took a step forward, hands held out, his eyes never leaving the gun. "She has nothing to do with this. Whatever you want, you can take it from me. Just let her go."

Victor's lips curled into a twisted smile. "Oh, she has everything to do with this, mate," he said with cruel pleasure. "You took something from me. Now I'll take something from you."

Marica's heart sank. Edward had always been the one to talk his way out of situations, to find a way through the impossible. But this time, she felt it—the helplessness in his eyes. There was no way out this time. Not without a price.

"If it's money you want…" Edward's voice was strained, each word heavier than the last. "I'll get it. Just let her go."

Victor's eyes narrowed. "Money? You think I'm here for money, Edward? You always were good at talking, weren't you? Not this time."

Marica's voice trembled as she turned her head to look at Edward. "Edward, don't listen to him. He's lying… he'll kill us both," she pleaded, her eyes desperate.

Victor laughed, a cruel, guttural sound. His fingers dug deeper into her wrist as he pulled her closer. "Smart woman," he whispered, his breath hot against her ear. But there was nothing but cold in his words.

Without warning, Edward lunged.

A blur of motion followed. Marica was thrown to the floor as the two men struggled, the gun swinging wildly in their fight. Edward's arm was grazed by the metal, but he fought to get closer to her, to free her from Victor's grasp. The air was thick with fear as Marica scrambled away, her body colliding with the cold, hard floor.

Bang!

The sharp, violent crack of gunfire split the tension in the room.

Bang!

Another shot.

Marica's breath caught as her vision swam. The acrid scent of gunpowder filled her nostrils, choking her. In a daze, she looked toward Edward. His body was slumped to the floor, blood already pooling beneath him.

"Edward!" Her voice shattered the silence, filled with raw panic.

But he didn't respond.

Her heart pounded in her chest as she scrambled to her feet, ignoring the pain that shot through her head. She crawled toward him, desperation flooding her every move. When she reached him, she turned him over, the sight of his blood-soaked shirt making her stomach lurch.

"No... no, no..." she whispered, her hands shaking uncontrollably as she pressed them against his chest. The blood was already soaking through, spreading like a dark, irreversible stain. "Edward, please... stay with me..."

But then—

A sharp gasp.

A ragged inhale.

Marica froze. Her breath caught in her throat as she watched Edward's eyes flutter open, weak but still alive. His voice was barely more than a whisper, laced with his trademark teasing smirk. "Lucky for me," he rasped, lifting his shirt to reveal the bulletproof vest beneath. "I came prepared."

Relief flooded her chest like a wave. Her hands trembled as she cupped his face, tears slipping from her eyes. "You idiot," she whispered, her voice breaking. "I thought… I thought I lost you."

Edward smiled faintly, even though the pain, his thumb gently brushing away a tear from her cheek. "You love this idiot," he murmured, the humour still there despite the blood on his hands.

But the moment of relief was short-lived.

A scream pierced the air—a woman's scream.

Marica turned just as Rachel, standing near the door, crumpled to the ground. Her body jerked violently as she fell, blood blossoming from her chest in a dark red stain. Marica's heart stopped.

"Rachel!" Marica screamed, rushing toward her.

Victor stood not far behind her, his eyes filled with cold fury. He hadn't even flinched when Rachel collapsed. His jaw was clenched tight, his face twisted with anger and betrayal. "You think I'd just forget?" he spat, stepping forward. "You were supposed to be loyal, Rachel. You turned your back on me... Now, you pay for that."

Rachel's lifeless eyes stared up at the ceiling, shock and disbelief still etched on her face. She had betrayed Victor, and in his mind, this was the price she had to pay.

Victor's gaze turned back to Marica, his fury still burning bright. "She thought she could play me, and now she's dead because of it. Just like you would be, if I hadn't been so careful." His words dripped with venom, every syllable soaked in the bitterness of revenge.

Marica's breath caught in her throat as she fell to her knees beside Rachel's body. This was the ultimate betrayal. Rachel had gotten involved with Victor's schemes, deceiving him—and in turn, sealing her own fate.

Victor didn't even seem to care about what he'd done, his cold eyes still fixated on Marica. The sirens were getting closer, but the damage was already done.

The front door burst open just as Victor was turning to leave. The police had arrived. Detective Thomas and his team rushed through the back door, their weapons drawn, quickly surrounding Victor and his men.

"You're under arrest for the murder of Rachel, conspiracy, fraud, and organized crime," Detective Thomas announced, his voice firm and unwavering.

Victor's eyes blazed with fury, but there was nothing left to do. He was outnumbered, overpowered. He snarled as he was cuffed and dragged away.

But Marica couldn't focus on him. Not now. Not when Rachel's life had just been taken.

As Victor was led away, Marica turned back to Edward, her hand trembling as she gripped his. His eyes were tired, but they locked with hers, offering her a semblance of comfort.

"We did it," she said softly, her voice raw from everything that had happened.

Edward squeezed her hand, his arm wrapping around her shoulders in a protective embrace. "We did."

But in the pit of her stomach, Marica knew that victory had come at a price. Rachel's blood was on the floor, and though they had broken free from Victor's grip, the cost was more than she was ready to face.

And as the weight of everything pressed down on her, she realized that while this moment was a victory, it was also the beginning of a long journey—a journey of healing, of loss, and of the painful but necessary road to forgiveness. But for the first time in a long while, Marica allowed herself to feel something she hadn't in months: hope.

Chapter 30: A Miracle in the Making

The ambulance ride felt like a distant memory, an eternity of flashing lights and sirens, yet everything around Marica seemed to blur in slow motion. Her hands trembled uncontrollably, her body too exhausted to calm down. She gripped Edward's hand tightly, as if her grip could somehow anchor her to the world, to him, to the reality that she had made it this far.

But then came the pain—the first sharp contraction. It tore through her, so fierce it stole her breath.

"Edward…" she gasped, her fingers squeezing his palm with all the strength she had left.

His face twisted with concern, but there was no time for fear. "Marica, look at me. Focus on me. Breathe. In and out."

Another wave of pain hit, stronger this time. She squeezed her eyes shut, trying to centre herself, but the waves of agony kept coming.

The paramedic, his voice calm yet urgent, looked up at them. "She's in labour."

"No," Marica whispered in disbelief, the words barely escaping her lips. "It's too soon. Three months… too soon."

Edward's face paled, but his grip on her hand never wavered. "I know, love. But we're going to get through this. Breathe."

But there was no time for calm. No time for reassurance. The next few hours became a blur of bright lights, the constant hum of machines, and the chaotic rush of doctors and nurses around her. Everything seemed a thousand miles away, like she was floating above it all, watching as her life—and the life of their daughter—hung in the balance.

Edward wasn't allowed inside the operating room, and Marica's heart broke as she was wheeled away from him. He paced the hallway, his mind spinning, his pulse racing faster than the seconds on the clock. Every minute felt like an hour, every tick a reminder of how fragile life could be.

And then, after what seemed like a lifetime, it came.

A cry.

A sharp, piercing wail that sliced through the tension and the fear, the sound of life—of hope.

The doctor emerged from the operating room, his expression one of cautious relief. "She's here. Your daughter. She's here."

Edward let out a shaky breath, the weight of the moment crashing into him like a tidal wave. "And Marica? Is she...?"

"She's stable. They both are."

His heart lifted in a way he hadn't thought possible. He barely heard the doctor's words as he rushed past him into the room.

There, in the sterile quiet of the hospital, he saw her—Marica. Exhausted, her face pale, but there was a light in her eyes as she cradled the tiny bundle in her arms. A miracle.

His breath caught in his throat as he walked toward her, reaching out to gently brush a damp lock of hair from her forehead. She looked up at him, and there was a softness in her gaze that made his heart swell. "She's beautiful," he whispered.

Marica's eyes glistened with unshed tears, and for a moment, it felt like the world stood still. "She's our Elizabeth," she murmured. "Born too soon... but strong. A fighter. Just like us."

Edward's chest tightened, emotion choking him. He didn't know what he'd expected, but it wasn't this. A tiny, fragile life—one he wasn't sure they'd get to hold—was now in their arms, defying the odds. And, somehow, so was she. Marica was here. She was alive. They had made it.

And in that moment, Edward knew. No matter the battles they'd faced, no matter the struggles yet to come, they had this. They had each other. And they had their miracle.

Chapter 31: A New Beginning

News travelled fast. Within hours of hearing the news, Marica's mother, Nancy, had booked a flight from Singapore. She arrived at the hospital with a face etched in worry, but the moment she laid eyes on her daughter and granddaughter, the concern melted away, replaced by tears of joy.

"She's perfect," Nancy whispered, cradling little Elizabeth in her arms as if she was the most precious thing in the world. "Just perfect."

The days that followed were a blur of settling into a new rhythm, one that included caring for a fragile, tiny life and adjusting to the reality of their new normal. Every moment was a delicate balance of joy and exhaustion, but it was theirs to embrace.

Meanwhile, Victor was taken to a separate hospital under heavy police guard. His injuries, though serious, weren't life-threatening. The man who had brought so much pain to their lives would face the consequences of his actions. After months of recovery, he was convicted of attempted murder, conspiracy, and organized crime. The sentence was handed down—fifteen years behind bars.

With Victor's fate sealed, Edward and Marica felt a sense of peace they hadn't known in months. They had come through the storm, and now, they could finally breathe.

They returned to Cornwall, where they began to rebuild the life they had worked so hard to create. Their restaurant, a symbol of their perseverance, continued to thrive, becoming a beacon of stability for their little family. With Nancy by their side, caring for Elizabeth with all the tenderness and love of a grandmother, Edward and Marica found themselves adjusting to a quieter, more grounded life. It wasn't without its challenges, but it was theirs.

Yet, despite the sense of peace that had settled over them, there was a quiet, unspoken longing—one that neither of them could shake. Singapore.

It wasn't just a city. It was home. It was Marica's birthplace, her roots, her history. And though Edward had once been an outsider, he had come to love the city as his own, drawn in by its pulse, its contradictions, and its beauty. They both knew that one day, they would return.

Not just for them, but for Elizabeth.

She deserved to know the city that had shaped her mother. To walk down the bustling streets, to experience the blend of the old and the new—modern skyscrapers rising against the backdrop of ancient temples. She deserved to learn about her cultural heritage, the traditions that had been passed down through generations.

They knew they couldn't give her the world all at once, but they could give her the future they had fought so hard for. So, they did what they always did: worked. Every extra penny they earned from the restaurant went into a savings fund, a nest egg for their future in Singapore. It was a future filled with the promise of the best education, the best opportunities, and a life brimming with the possibilities that only the city could offer.

For now, though, they held on to what they had. The sound of Elizabeth's tiny coos, the warmth of a family finally at peace, and the knowledge that no matter how far their journey took them, they would always find their way back to each other.

Because home wasn't just a place.

It was family.

And with Elizabeth nestled in their arms, Edward and Marica knew that no matter where they went, as long as they were together, they were home.

Chapter 32: The Long Road Home

The time had come. After years of building a life together in Cornwall—years marked by love, loss, and triumph—Edward and Marica made the monumental decision to return to Singapore. Their daughter, Elizabeth, was now eighteen, standing on the precipice of adulthood, ready to embark on a new journey of her own. University life awaited her in the city that had once been Marica's home, and now, it was about to become Elizabeth's.

How time changes everything.

Singapore, once a quiet fishing village, had transformed into one of the most breathtakingly vibrant cities in the world. It had embraced modernity without losing its soul. The skyline was a magnificent tapestry of glass and steel, with icons like Marina Bay Sands and the Supertree Grove standing tall against the sky. Orchard Road shimmered with lights, and the pulse of the city vibrated with the energy of its people. It was a city that had reinvented itself, a place where tradition and innovation coexisted, but its essence—its heart—remained unchanged.

With a mixture of sadness and excitement, they sold their beloved business in Cornwall, the place where so many memories had been made and used the proceeds to purchase a cozy condo in Balestier, just a stone's throw from the peaceful Novena Church. It felt right. It felt like a new beginning, a new chapter in their story.

As they settled into their new home, Elizabeth sat by the window, gazing out at the streets of Singapore. The city, so full of life, seemed to hold endless possibilities. She turned to her parents, her curiosity burning bright.

"Mum, Dad... how did you two really meet?" she asked, her voice laced with a kind of wonder that only a daughter could have when trying to understand the love story of her parents.

Marica's gaze softened as the memories washed over her. "It was by fate," she began, her voice tinged with the magic of the moment. "We were strangers passing by each other, lost in the rush of Changi Airport, when somehow... we just looked at each other."

Edward smiled at the memory, his eyes filled with warmth. "It wasn't much more than a glance, but when she smiled—her smile—it changed everything. In that instant, I knew something had shifted."

Marica's eyes twinkled, and she continued, her voice light and wistful. "It was a smile that felt like an invitation, as if the universe itself whispered, 'This is where it all begins.'"

Elizabeth's heart fluttered as she listened. "You were just passing by, and yet that smile brought you together?"

Edward nodded slowly, his voice filled with quiet awe. "Yes. Sometimes, all it takes is one moment—a single glance, a single smile—and everything changes."

Elizabeth leaned forward, her excitement palpable. "I want to write about it. Your story, your journey. Everything. I want people to understand that love can find you in the most unexpected ways."

Edward's smile deepened, a mixture of pride and affection. "Then write it, sweetheart. Share our story with the world."

And so, as the sun dipped behind the skyline, casting a golden glow over the city, a new chapter began for all of them. A chapter filled with new memories, new adventures, and a future that was waiting to be written.

The Long Road Home was not just a title, it was their story, and it was still unfolding. The road they had travelled had led them here, to this moment, and now they would walk forward together, hand in hand, into the unknown, ready to create the next beautiful part of their journey.

www.ingramcontent.com/pod-product-compliance
Ingram Content Group UK Ltd.
Pitfield, Milton Keynes, MK11 3LW, UK
UKHW010754080126
9979UKWH00019B/65